This was too soon, too fast. She wasn't ready yet.

Would she ever have been, though?

Lucie had known this time would come. She'd known it had to. It was only right. But she'd never thought it would come almost the minute she arrived in town.

Distressed, she stared, her stomach knotted, and she felt as though the blood in her veins had turned to ice. Everything around her slowed. The brilliant Pacific Northwest blues and piney emerald-greens faded to gray. Nothing existed but the man staring at her, holding her shoulders.

Lucie stood frozen in place, staring into the uncannily familiar blue-gray eyes, eyes her daughter had inherited from…

From the man before her.

The man Lucie hadn't seen in six years, hadn't managed to find in all that time. The man she'd finally located in Washington State.

The man she'd traveled across the continent to introduce to his daughter.

Books by Ginny Aiken

Love Inspired

The Daddy Surprise

Love Inspired Suspense

Mistaken for the Mob
Mixed up with the Mob
Married to the Mob
*Danger in a Small Town
*Suspicion
*Someone to Trust

*Carolina Justice

GINNY AIKEN

Born in Havana, Cuba, raised in Valencia and Caracas, Venezuela, Ginny Aiken discovered books early and wrote her first novel at age fifteen while she trained with the Ballets de Caracas, later known as the Venezuelan National Ballet. She burned that tome when she turned a "mature" sixteen. Stints as reporter, paralegal, choreographer, language teacher and retail salesperson followed. Her life as wife, mother of four boys and herder of their numerous and assorted friends brought her back to books and writing in search of her sanity. She's now the author of more than twenty published works and a frequent speaker at Christian women's and writers' workshops, but has yet to catch up with that elusive sanity.

The Daddy Surprise

Ginny Aiken

Love Inspired

PLEASE RECYCLE · THIS PRODUCT IS RECYCLABLE ·

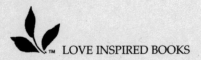 ™ LOVE INSPIRED BOOKS

Recycling programs
for this product may
not exist in your area.

ISBN-13: 978-0-373-87683-9

THE DADDY SURPRISE

Copyright © 2011 by Grisel Anikienko

www.LoveInspiredBooks.com

Printed in U.S.A.

I will restore to you the years
that the swarming locust has eaten...
—*Joel* 2:25

To my youngest son, Grant, our Comeback Kid.
You're my hero.

Chapter One

I will restore to you the years that the swarming locust has eaten...

Joel 2:25

Lyndon Point, Washington State

Lucie Adams slammed on the brakes.

A car honked behind her.

The sight of the crumbling Victorian at the corner of Main and Sea Breeze Way stole her breath.

"Ma-*maaaa!*"

When the panic in her five-year-old daughter's voice registered, she murmured, "Sorry, Chloe, honey. It's okay. You can relax."

Lucie stared some more. Then, wearing a satisfied grin, she eased her foot off the brake.

So far so good.

As she rounded the corner, excitement bubbled inside her. She continued to stare in her rearview mirror at the house—the very shabby, once-upon-a-time magnificent Queen Anne Victorian she had discovered on this, her first drive through her soon-to-be new hometown.

The house was perfect, but it needed so much work. She only had five months' worth of funds in her savings account. She'd thought that would see her through, but now…she'd need to make it stretch. She'd have to rethink the pricey extended-stay suite hotel where she and Chloe were rooming.

Her excitement grew.

Up ahead, real estate agent Edna Lyndon's zippy, red convertible continued down the street. In her final peek in the mirror as she followed Edna, Lucie spied the corner of the wraparound porch, the turret above, the rusted iron fence hemming in the overgrown garden, and fell totally in love.

"It's perfect," she whispered.

While the place was a mess, with peeling paint, faded and sagging shutters, broken gingerbread trim on the porch and missing fish-scale shingles on the pitched peak of the turret, Lucie knew she could turn the place into the home of her dreams—

Nope! I don't have to turn it into anything.

The Victorian already *was* the home of her dreams. Lucie wanted a fixer-upper with lots of character for her and Chloe to live in, and to be the site for her new endeavor, the quilt and fabric shop she planned to open in Lyndon Point. This bedraggled treasure would clean up great.

Her heartbeat sped up and hope kicked into high gear. She couldn't wait to ask Edna about the place.

The sixty-something Realtor pulled into a small, crowded parking lot on Sea Breeze Way, across from the Victorian on the corner. Lucie followed. As they crawled past the lines of cars, they found an empty spot—the only one—in the farthest row. Edna gestured for Lucie to roll down her window.

"You take this one, dear," she called out. "Shirley Wilcox will let me park behind her Tea & Sympathy shop about a block away—it's a wonderful little place. You'll have to stop in when you get a chance." She waved toward the parking spot. "Go ahead. Take this one. It'll only take a minute for me to get back. I'll meet you girls inside."

Since Lucie had to wrestle her hungry five-year-old out of the booster seat and herd her into the diner, one of those complex mothering maneuvers she performed hourly, she thanked Edna and focused on squeezing in between the SUVs on either side of the parking space. She grabbed her purse, freed Chloe, gripped the little hand and turned toward the quaint eatery.

At Lucie's side Chloe hippety-hopped, her pink sun hat flopping along, practically swallowing her little face in its shadow. Chloe loved the hat. Lucie? Not so much. But in view of their cross-country move to Washington State and all the disruption it had forced on the five-year-old, Lucie figured the hat wasn't worth a battle.

"Mama! I want chicken nuggets." Chloe rarely whined, but she was coming close now. "D'you think they got—"

"They *have,* Chloe."

"Oh, goody! That's what I want. With barber cube sauce."

Sigh. "I don't know if they have chicken nuggets. I meant the right way to say it is 'Do you think they *have,*' not 'D'you think they got'—"

"But, Mama!" Chloe's voice rose in pitch and volume. "It's all the same."

"The meaning may be the same, but how you say it matters, too."

Chloe yanked her hand free, crossed her arms and squared her chin. She glared, and when Lucie didn't react immediately, she stomped over to the bubblegum dispenser at the left of the diner's door. But Chloe rarely forgot an ultimate goal. "I want nuggets," she shot over her shoulder. "With barber cube sauce."

Lucie got down to her hungry and cranky daughter's level. "I can't promise nuggets with *barbecue* sauce. They might have them, and they might not. But I know they'll have at least one yummy lunch choice for you. And, after we eat, how about we go down to the beach?"

Chloe's distinctive blue-gray eyes widened. "The beach?"

"Mmm-hmm. We can go right after we eat."

"Can we swim?"

"Oh, I don't think you want to do that. The water here's awfully cold." Lucie straightened and, grabbing Chloe's hand again, turned toward the diner's door. "Let's check it out—*oof!*"

She'd crashed into a wall. With hands. That held her by the shoulders. Kept her from falling. Sent shivers right through her. "I'm so sorry...."

As she looked up, her stomach took a sickening dive. Her words dried in her throat.

Oh, no. Nonononono—

This was too soon, too fast. She wasn't ready yet.

Would she ever have been?

From the moment she'd seen the mayor's picture on the Lyndon Point webpage, Lucie had known this time would come.

She never thought it would come almost the minute she arrived.

She stared, her stomach knotted and she felt as though the blood in her veins had turned to ice. Everything around her slowed. The brilliant blues and piney emerald greens of the Pacific Northwest faded to gray. Nothing existed but the man staring at her, holding her shoulders.

Long, strained seconds oozed by. Lucie felt the urge to run, to grab Chloe and hide her, to protect her daughter from the potential pain she might face. But she couldn't run. She had nowhere to go. This was why she'd come so far, the real reason behind her move.

Lucie stood frozen in place, staring into the familiar blue-gray eyes, eyes her daughter had inherited from…

From the man before her.

The man Lucie hadn't seen in six years, hadn't managed to find in all that time. The guy she'd finally located in Washington State.

She'd crossed the continent to introduce him to his daughter.

An eternity later, the warmth of his strong, steady hands penetrated the chill in Lucie. Among the myriad of emotions at odds within her, she identified one she hadn't expected. Yearning opened up, tugged at her, teased her memory, reminding her of the fragile new love she'd once felt.

For him.

No! She couldn't go there. That all had died the day—

Lucie shuddered, breaking the spell he'd cast on her. Eyes glued to the face from her past, she longed for the time she'd hoped to have to prepare herself and Chloe, but that had now vanished. Her past and her present had collided.

"Ryder," she whispered.

Confusion crossed his features. His intense eyes narrowed. A hint of a smile brightened the ruggedly handsome features when he made the connection. "Cindy…?"

As his rich baritone voice sounded out the name no one else called her, Lucie tried to draw breath, but her lungs felt squeezed dry. She shook her head, unable to tear her gaze away from the man she'd never forgotten. She wanted to speak, but knew nothing would come out.

"My mama's not Cindy, mister. She's Lucie. Lucie Adams."

Ryder's blue-gray gaze shot down to Chloe. His eyes widened in shock, homed in on the little girl.

In the long, slow moments that followed, he continued to stare, from Lucie to Chloe, who'd moved back to the bubblegum machine. His jaw gaped. He snapped it shut and narrowed his gaze.

That icy stare lasered into her. "Her...*mama?*"

Lucie stepped between Ryder and Chloe to protect her daughter, if only momentarily. She tipped up her chin. "Yes."

He ran a hand down his face, drew in a rough breath, pinned her with a piercing glare. "I don't need my accounting degree to do this kind of math. I might not know much about little kids, but what's adding up here doesn't take a genius to figure out. You really do flit around like the butterfly you once said you felt like. Didn't take you long to replace me, did it?"

Lucie felt gut-punched, hurt to the very core. She shook her head, fought back the tears, but because Chloe was with them, she couldn't argue in her own defense.

Before she could muster the strength to speak, Ryder broke the long silence with a hard, cold voice. "How old is she?"

Lucie pulled herself together. She stiffened her spine, drew back her shoulders, aiming for a bravado she didn't feel. "Five."

Chloe poked her head around the side of Lucie's hip. "I'm s'more months more'n that."

Ryder's jaw tightened and his Adam's apple jerked as he swallowed. "And your *mother's* name is...Lucie?"

The floppy hat bobbed as Chloe nodded three times.

Lucie hated the emotional currents eddying around her, the sadness, the anger, the heartache.

Time to get a grip.

Who cared if her heart beat harder than an orchestra's gong or whether she could barely squeeze air into or out from her lungs? She wasn't so much a coward as to let her daughter speak for her. Not now, not to him, not about this.

She met Ryder's gaze full-on. "My name is Lucinda Marie Adams. I go by Lucie rather than Cindy. I always have."

A muscle in his granite jaw twitched again. "Not always."

Her heart threatened to fail, and her cheeks burned. No, she hadn't called herself Lucie when they'd met. She'd thought it so chic, so sophisticated to have no past, only a present that allowed for a wild, spontaneous week without strings.

In her mind, a Cindy had felt more like the carefree woman who would have that kind of vacation. Lucie, on the other hand, was a woman burdened with a family's spiderweb of duty and expectations. The memories—*no!*

She couldn't afford those memories. "You're right. I didn't go by my name that week. But, Ryder, you didn't, either. The town website said your name is—"

"Matthew Ryder Lyndon." His eyes lighted on her face before it darted to a nearby tree. He looked at the blue sky, the diner's door—anywhere but at her. "No, it's not the same. Not really."

As she waited for his explanation, his hands fisted. He cleared his throat. "You see, everyone's always called me Ryder. Matthew's my legal name, of course, so I use it for official business and legal documents like driver's license, passport, the mayor's webpage...."

To her surprise, the confident athlete she remembered had gone missing. The adult and obviously uncomfortable Ryder slipped his hands in his pockets, shrugged. "I am—I mean…I've been Ryder my whole life."

Lucie clamped her lips tight to keep from speaking. She wasn't ready to say anything, didn't want to blurt out something that might make things worse. It appeared their encounter was rattling him as much as it was her. His rambling explanation revealed…something. She hoped it meant he recognized his part in the mix-up.

As soon as she'd seen the mayor's page on the Lyndon Point website, she'd realized the middle-name thing explained why she'd failed every time she'd tried to find him. No one by the name of Ryder had been registered at any Baja hotel. Nor had any Ryder made airline reservations, either. Now Matthew Lyndon, Matthew R. Lyndon, M. R. Lyndon…? Any of those might have, but she hadn't known to look for them, and the people she'd asked hadn't volunteered any more information than they'd had to.

Ryder had hidden his identity, blurred it by the use of his middle name, if not necessarily on purpose. It wasn't *that* different from what she'd done. Not really…

Well, maybe it was. She'd given him a different version of her name, one she'd adopted that spring vacation her senior year in college for the sake of an out-of-character, superficial encounter.

Lucie sighed. She could do nothing to change the past now. All she could do was commit to make the future better.

As though from a great distance, an insistent voice penetrated the haze around them. "Ma-*maaaaa!*"

They both turned to Chloe. Lucie took advantage of the distraction to escape the unnerving warmth of Ryder's gaze. She'd missed his presence when they'd parted years ago. After that week of almost constant closeness, the loneliness that had enveloped her when they'd parted had eased over time, but seeing Ryder again... He hadn't changed much, and the pull of attraction surprised her.

A lump filled her throat.

She swallowed hard against it.

As she faced her little girl, she reminded herself that those memories and feelings didn't belong in the moment. All of that could wait until she felt less vulnerable and until the time was right. For her daughter, of course.

Right then, Lucie had something more urgent to deal with. Like nuggets with barber cube sauce.

"I'm sorry, Chloe," she said. "I know you're hungry, but I took a few minutes to say hello to—" she glanced up, but the look on Ryder's face made her turn back to her daughter right away "—the gentleman. I'm done now, so let's go eat."

With Chloe's hand back in her clasp, and the hat casting its protective shadow over the child's face, she stood and stepped toward the door.

One of Ryder's warm hands dropped onto her shoulder again. "Not so fast."

She slanted him a glance, fighting hard not to show how much his touch unsettled her. "Yes?"

"Don't you think we have plenty more to discuss? Like your vanishing act—" he shot a pointed look at Chloe "—among other things?"

He was right. They did have plenty to discuss. Like his own silence at their parting. And the promiscuity of which he'd accused her. She could see how someone, a stranger looking at their one-week relationship, who didn't know the truth about Chloe, might come to that conclusion. But she would have thought Ryder had come to know her better than that even in just their short time together.

"You're right," she said. "We do have a lot to discuss. I knew we would when I decided to come to Lyndon Point. You're…umm…one of the reasons I'm moving here. But I'm sure you can see this isn't the best time to go into that."

His face revealed the many questions he had. But he only nodded in response. "Of course. What do you suggest?"

"That we meet later or another day. When we can talk, try to catch up."

Five years of Chloe's existence were going to take a whole lot of catching up, much longer than one simple dinner might last. That was why Lucie intended to move to Lyndon Point. While she could open her quilt shop in any of dozens of small towns, only one, Lyndon Point, offered her the chance to make up for some of the harm her thoughtlessness years ago had caused.

Once she and Chloe settled into their new place, Lucie and Ryder would have all the time they'd need to talk. To clear up old issues. Most importantly, to share their child.

She shuddered.

After another brief silence, he shrugged. "You name the time, but don't put it off. That conversation's long overdue." His look gave her no wiggle room. "Right about six years overdue."

"I didn't know where to find you.…"

The icy light in those blue-gray eyes didn't thaw one degree.

Lucie reminded herself to breathe. In…out, in…out.

Now that they'd come face-to-face again, and she confronted his anger, she wasn't so sure she was ready to peel back the tender tissue over the wound their too-brief relationship had left. She didn't know if she could go through that pain again.

But Ryder wanted to talk. And, to be fair, it was time to put everything on the table.

"Dinner," she said, glad her voice resembled something close to normal. "How about dinner tonight? I think I can arrange for a sitter at my hotel."

"I'll see you at six-thirty. Right here. We'll figure out where to eat at that time."

As he spun on his heel, Chloe called out, "G'bye, mister!"

Ryder paused, looked over his shoulder, the harsh angle of his tight jaw and the cold gleam in his eyes a clear reflection of his response to their sudden encounter. But as he studied Chloe, so sweet in her princess-pink outfit and floppy hat, for whose cover Lucie was truly grateful, the glare in his eyes began a slow thaw. A hint of a smile relaxed the hard line of his clamped lips.

Here, in this smiling, approachable man Lucie found the Ryder she fell for all that time ago.

Suppressed tears scalded her eyes.

Ryder took a step toward Chloe, tapped the brim of the hat with one hand, held the other one out and took the child's small fingers in his. "Goodbye, Chloe. I'm sure you'll like your lunch. I'll see you soon."

He walked away, his steps long and smooth, still as athletic as when he'd told Lucie about his college basketball career. She watched, the old ache growing, her heart pounding in her chest, her pulse throbbing in her temples.

This was the man who'd stolen her heart during a crazy, uncharacteristic week of rebellion her senior year in college. He'd been gentle, caring and oh-so-charming. Handsome…strong. A dream partner for an exciting spring-break fling.

While at first Lucie had tried to have that sophisticated, no-strings romance, she'd soon realized she wasn't the no-strings kind. She'd fallen head-over-heels for Ryder. But when it was time to return to Houston for the last few weeks of school, he hadn't said a thing about feelings, the future or anything else. He'd stared at her with a smoldering light in those amazing eyes of his, held her tight in his embrace for a too-short moment and opened his arms to let her go her way.

She'd had no alternative but to take herself and her broken heart back to her old life. She'd tried to forget, to return to her normal routine.

But when she'd left the Baja Peninsula, she'd taken with her more than memories and a broken heart. She'd taken their daughter in her womb.

Chapter Two

Ｈow he made it back to his office, Ryder would never know. His thoughts raced, and he felt as though a prize-fighter had landed a right hook to his jaw. Cindy...

After all this time. In Lyndon Point.

Cindy—Lucie. Lucie, she'd said. Same golden-brown-haired, hazel-eyed woman, different name.

Mother of a little girl...

Of Chloe.

With his mouth as dry as a dissertation on tax law, he made his way down Main Street, not noticing much of anything. Even his constituents' greetings faded into a blur in the background. Thoughts tumbled in his head, random images that intruded into every effort to put his past and this new reality in perspective. He failed each time. Perspective didn't come easy when a man was plain, old stunned.

While he'd never given up all hope of someday coming across Cindy again, he had reached a point where he'd accepted facts. For all practical purposes, and Ryder considered himself the most practical of men, Cindy was gone, even though the memories and lingering hurt weren't. Not completely.

Then—*bam!* She'd crashed into him, and those old feelings had rushed right back.

Not to mention, the sudden shot of jealousy he'd felt toward Chloe's father, whoever he might be.

Sensible, practical, logical Ryder was irrationally jealous of a guy he hadn't even met. He couldn't suppress the spurt of anger each time he thought of Cindy with another man. And so soon after they'd parted.

He supposed he'd have to get over it, since he'd more than likely be seeing her around town. With the man. With Chloe.

All those years he'd wondered about Cindy—*Lucie*—she'd been raising a child, molding a young life. In contrast, building the career he loved so much now paled in magnitude. He couldn't help but wonder what kind of life he would have built if he'd been a father to someone like Chloe.

A rogue thought crossed his mind. Could he have been—could he *be*—Chloe's father?

They'd been careful. Very careful.

Still, the timing…

Possible? Sure. Likely? Not so much.

Right?

But that meant that, after their time together, Cindy had walked away and replaced Ryder quickly. With Chloe's father.

Still in a haze, he walked into his office. On a normal day, the warm gold walls and brown leather furniture welcomed him, blanketed him with a sense of pride in all his achievements. Today, he might as well have walked into the DMV to replace his driver's license.

He zoned in on the door to his personal office. As he went to closet himself in his private haven, his assistant's voice caught his attention. Wendy must have been speaking to him from the moment he'd walked in.

"...and Homer Magnusson wants to meet with you to discuss Council's decision on his zoning petition." She slapped down the last pink message slip on the substantial pile before her and shoved it all toward him.

As she waited for his response, which was much slower than usual in coming, Wendy tapped an electric-yellow notepad with her yellow, banana slug–shaped pen. She pushed her rimless glasses up her nose, not high enough to conceal her arched eyebrow.

"Oh, yeah," she added. "There's also your aunt Myra. She says she *neeeeeeeds* to see you. Says it's urgent, and you can't put her off anymore. You're to call her to arrange a time to meet."

With one hand, Wendy raked her short, dark auburn hair; with the other, she picked up her yellow mug, decorated with the outline of a banana slug. An alumna of the University of California in Santa Cruz, Wendy took the school's yellow banana slug mascot—a disgusting creature all too common in the Pacific Northwest—way too seriously. Most days, his assistant's devotion struck him as funny. Today, it barely registered.

Like whatever she'd told him a moment earlier. "I'm sorry. What'd you say about Aunt Myra?"

Both eyebrows shot up over the lenses. "You okay, Boss?"

He shrugged. "Yep. Just dan—" He cut off his sarcastic response to replace it with a mild "Fine."

Wendy handed him the thick wad of messages, stressing the urgency of Aunt Myra's call one more time.

Like the rest of his relatives, his late father's younger sister counted on Ryder to resolve her business woes and mishaps. From time to time, her family issues, too. And, as all his extended family members did when they turned to him with their problems, she needed his help *now*.

This time, however, "now" wasn't going to work. Ryder had something more urgent to deal with at the moment.

And yet, he still had his business to run. He had the town to administer. He couldn't set all that aside because his life had taken a hike down Alice's rabbit hole and come out into an alternate reality.

Like Aunt Myra, a lot of people depended on him. These days, Ryder was a responsible man, an adult, no longer the college senior who'd indulged in the one and only spontaneous fling of his life with a girl who'd wanted no strings.

A girl who'd soon moved on to the next guy.

And Chloe.

For Ryder that week had become more than just a vacation. It had turned into much more than a romantic fling. That week had become one of the most important learning experiences of his life.

The first thing he had learned was how deeply he could care, how hard and fast he could fall and how long the experience would stay with him.

Ryder had also realized he appreciated boring but reliable virtues, character qualities like responsibility and duty, commitment and dedication. He'd learned that spontaneity had its place, but that its freedom, self-indulgence and turmoil left him craving the measure of control, certainty and discipline he needed for personal satisfaction and general success. In the end, he'd learned he wasn't a "fling" kind of guy. He wanted the long-term, the house and mortgage and forever kind of deal.

Faster than he might have imagined, Ryder had come to want more from Cindy than she'd seemed willing to give. He'd wanted more tomorrows, maybe even that future with her. He'd wanted to explore where the long talks, shared laughs, the common and the not-so-common interests, and the easy companionship might lead. But when her vacation had come to an end, Cindy hadn't said a word about the future. On their last day together she'd burrowed into his chest for a final embrace and, after giving him a sweet, sad smile topped with damp eyes, hurried to catch up with her friends.

Ryder was left with vivid memories and a broken heart.

How could something so brief hurt so much when it ended?

Ryder ran a hand through his hair. Why had he not been able to get over that week? After all, it had been *only* a week. Time and time again, he'd called himself all kinds of stupid for thinking back to Cindy and that handful of sunny days as often as he did.

Now he could really call himself stupid. She clearly hadn't treasured their time together as much as he had. After all, she'd turned to someone else pretty fast after they'd parted. And while it shouldn't, the thought of Cindy—*Lucie*. It was time to think of the woman at the diner as Lucie, not the "Cindy" of his past. Maybe then the thought of her with another man wouldn't make anger simmer to life, as had happened when she'd introduced him to her little girl. Hers and some other guy's little girl.

Lucie had borne another man's child. She'd spent the last five years raising someone else's daughter. He, instead, had wasted six years putting back together his broken heart, and protecting himself from a repeat of the pain their parting had caused.

In spite of all his efforts, he hadn't been able to avoid a whole lot more pain once he'd come home again. Two years after Cindy left him on a sunny beach, his much-loved sister walked, actually ran, away from him in anger. He'd looked for Deanna, done everything he could to try to find her, with no success.

After that, he hadn't had the stomach for any more desertions. He'd scrupulously avoided anything with even a whiff of romance.

Maybe his anger would finally help him put that vacation fling where it belonged: in the dead-and-buried past. He doubted he had enough pieces of himself left to put together again if he opened himself to more heartbreak.

Still, Ryder couldn't believe she'd crashed back into his life. With those warm honey-green eyes sadder than he remembered and that little girl in tow.

Cindy…er…Lucie, a mother. He couldn't quite fit the girl from his memories into his image of motherhood. The girl with whom he'd shared that intense week had been impulsive and spontaneous, lighthearted and without a care in the world. Not the top traits for a mother, in his opinion.

In spite of it all, he'd fallen for her. He'd wanted to know her better, he'd wanted to check out the possibility of a future, regardless of their differences. Even so, he'd held reservations about that potential future.

But he'd never envisioned a child in that future. Yet, here was Lucie, with a five-year-old.

Her little girl was five.

Once again his mind returned to the frightening possibility. He and Lucie *had* parted a few months less than six years ago. Was it possible? Could Chloe be his?

No. Of course not. She's not mine—can't be.

They had been very careful. Besides, if Chloe were his, Lucie would have moved heaven and earth to find him. Wouldn't she?

"Get a grip," he muttered. There hadn't been even a hint that there was any connection between Chloe and him.

A gust of breath ripped from his lungs. Oh, yeah. He and Lucie had a lot to discuss. And the topic wasn't going to be the notorious Pacific Northwest weather or the favorable business climate in Lyndon Point.

"So don't go and borrow more trouble by thinking insane stuff," he muttered to himself.

Adjusting to Lucie's presence in Lyndon Point would be trouble enough on top of his clients, his family responsibilities and mayoral duties.

Ryder forced his attention to the files on his desk. Because his personal world had been pitched off its steady, reliable base and onto its rear end didn't mean he could dump his business, or the town he'd been elected to run, into the same whirlpool.

But later, at dinner…dinner with Cindy—
Lucie.

Ryder had to put that new name to the face that had never been far from his thoughts. The face of the sun-washed girl he'd fallen for. The girl whose loss had brought him back home, to his roots and his faith, a changed man. The girl—woman—who'd now rocked his world again after almost six years.

Six years…time during which Ryder had fought to put things in perspective and learned how he preferred to lead his life. And how to succeed at anything he might take on. Especially since he'd failed so spectacularly at relationships.

He dropped into the comfortable leather chair behind his desk, both pieces of furniture perfectly suited to his long, lean frame. All the contents of his office worked well together. The chair not only fit him, but it also fit the size of his desk and the amount of space between the desk and the window behind it. The printer and copy machine sat in a discreet console against the left wall, and tall bookshelves full of tomes on economics, tax law, business and marketing theory, organized by author, topic and publication date, ran along the right wall. Everything had a spot. That was how he liked things. Organized, predictable, settled.

That was how he liked to work, too, in a methodical, detailed way. Control maximized efficiency.

Today, however, a whole lot of his hard-earned control had vanished. All because Lucie had come to town.

Yet another unsettling image invaded his thoughts, one he couldn't erase. All afternoon he struggled to concentrate on work while visions of an old TV show's scroll-lettered start-up screen danced in his head.

That vision stole the last of Ryder's peace of mind, since the original *I Love Lucy* morphed into a more personal and taunting message.

I love Lucie....

At the diner, as Lucie reached for the steel handle, the eatery's door flew open toward her. She stumbled back, her grip on Chloe's hand tight and protective.

Edna stuck her head outside, a twinkle in her gray eyes, her ultra-short, slightly spiked silver hair perfectly chic and flawlessly in place. "I slipped in the back door, dear." She bobbed her chin toward the departing Ryder. "Now, isn't that just like that boy? Welcoming the latest newcomers to town practically the minute you arrive. Our Ryder's about the finest mayor we've ever had. And so, so handsome! Don't you think?"

Edna's last name was also Lyndon. A crazy thought hit Lucie then. Could Edna be his mother? She was the right age, shared the last name. Not too far-fetched. And, wow! What were the odds that Lucie would have stumbled upon the woman who was also Chloe's grandmother?

Then again, that was too great a coincidence, even

though Edna was clearly related to Ryder. Lucie would have to check.

It occurred to her that working with Edna could become awkward at some point in the very near future.

A shudder shook her. What a day. What a morning it already had been.

As she led Chloe into the diner, she swallowed against the knot in her throat. The buzz of cheerful chitchat, the clatter of plates, fifties music, the succulent scents of meatloaf, chicken, cinnamon and sugar all melded together and embraced her before she'd gone more than three steps. The ambience of the place was pure comfort to Lucie's raw nerves. When she felt she could speak without betraying her raging emotions, she smiled at the Realtor.

"I've been curious. The mayor's last name is Lyndon, like yours. Are you related?"

Edna marched to a booth at the far right of the diner and scooted into a red vinyl corner. "He's my late brother Don's boy. I'll have you know, Ryder's the town's most eligible bachelor. But he's mighty picky when it comes to women. I suppose when a man's that prime a choice, he can be choosy. Tell me, now that you've met him, don't you think Ryder's the handsomest, nicest thing in trousers, button-down shirt and coordinated silk tie?"

Lucie squirmed under Edna's speculative stare. If she kept silent, she might come across as rude. If she answered...well, there was no good answer.

With a hefty dose of determination, Lucie dragged her attention back to Edna, who continued to praise the mayor and all his best qualities. Lucie knew better than anyone "what a catch some smart young lady would someday make, didn't she think?" But it wasn't up to her to comment.

It was, however, up to her to get her daughter fed. "Here's the menu, Chloe. Let's see what they have."

She sent Edna what she hoped came across as a natural smile, and concentrated on reading aloud the children's listings, hard though it was with her thoughts racing and her emotions churning her insides. Ryder always had that effect on her.

"Look at that, sweetie!" *Ugh.* She had to tone it down. Nobody got that excited about kids' lunch menus. "They *do* have chicken nuggets. How about some peas with those nuggets? And applesauce. You like that."

Chloe wrinkled her nose. "Peas? Do I hafta?"

Lucie touched her index finger to the upturned tip of her daughter's nose. "Yes, Ms. Chloe. You *hafta* have your veggies. They're good for you."

"But green's my most *un*-favorite color."

Edna chuckled while she studied Chloe, a thoughtful expression on her still-unlined face. With a somewhat skewed smile, she said, "Kids! I remember Don and Lila trying to get Ryder to eat his veggies, too. Quite a battle he put up, that little rascal."

Lucie gulped. Edna struck her as nobody's fool. And the Realtor had gotten a good look at Chloe, now that Lucie had taken off the child's hat. Those blue-gray eyes spoke volumes.

Had Edna figured it out? If so, what did she think? What would she think of Lucie…and about all those lost years of infancy and toddlerhood? How would she treat Chloe?

Another thought chased that one right out of Lucie's mind. She wasn't going to be able to keep Ryder's fatherhood a secret from anyone who saw her daughter. Before arriving in Lyndon Point, she'd known Chloe resembled her daddy. Today, however, Lucie had realized exactly how much their daughter looked like Ryder.

How would his constituents react? What were they going to think?

About him.

About her.

About Chloe, the innocent bystander.

She supposed she'd find out. And soon.

At Chloe's long-suffering sigh, Lucie dragged her thoughts back to the subject at hand. "Too bad about the green, Chloe-girl. And don't forget. We'll only go to the beach when you're done with lunch. That means finished with your meal. All of it. Even the peas."

Chloe sniffed and crossed her arms, a tiny line between her brows.

Edna hid behind her menu, but above the laminated list of choices, Lucie could see more laughter in the crinkled corners of her eyes. She was glad the Realtor had shielded her chuckles. There were times Lucie gave in to Chloe because the kiddo's antics hit her right and she couldn't ignore the funny side of the situation. She didn't know if she could have avoided snickering this time had Edna not been so discreet.

When the waitress came they placed their orders, and as they waited for the food, Lucie mentioned the wonderful, run-down Victorian. "It's perfect for my shop. And home."

Edna gulped down more than half of her fresh-squeezed lemonade. She picked up her BlackBerry, scrolled through her messages. She grabbed a warm roll from the basket, broke it into quarters, and buttered and honeyed them one by one before she finally nibbled tiny bites of the bread.

Lucie wasn't dumb. She got it. Edna didn't want to talk about the Victorian. But Lucie did. "Do you know who owns the house?"

Edna took another bite, this one larger. A muffled "Mmm-hmm" escaped in spite of the bread.

Lucie tried yet again. "It's obvious no one lives there."

A nervous smile tightened Edna's face as she nodded hard enough for her spikey hair to ripple with the motion.

The more Edna stonewalled, the more determined Lucie grew. "I'd like to tour the house. Whenever it's convenient. It's not as if someone would have to redo a schedule to let us into the place. With only one look, even a newcomer like me knows it's been vacant a very long time. My inspection wouldn't disturb anyone. I'm sure I can come up with terms that'll satisfy the owner. And me."

Edna's gray eyes opened wide. "Not in this lifetime!"

When she realized what she'd blurted out, she blushed. "I mean…the owner has no interest in selling. Period." She pushed a computer printout across the table. "Here's the information on the house you saw listed on our company's website. It's adorable, and I think it would be perfect for your store. I've arranged for us to see it this afternoon."

Lucie's instinct was to press on, but Edna's forced attention on the alternate property gave her no choice. She'd check out Edna's listing, but she'd also find a way to see the large Victorian. One way or another.

In the spirit of congeniality and the possibility that the cottage might work, Lucie read through the details. She agreed the place was attractive, with its white picket fence, pretty front porch and two neat dormer windows capping the roof. It could work. She'd give it a chance.

Mind made up, Lucie finished the last bit of her poached-salmon salad. "And you say we can see the cottage right away?"

The relief on Edna's face was almost comical. "Yes. Immediately."

Nodding like a dashboard bobblehead, a response at odds with the Realtor's casually chic appearance, Edna crammed her files and other papers back into a cordovan leather briefcase. "You'll see how perfect it is for you and Chloe—"

"Mama?"

"Yes, honey."

"The beach."

Oh, great. She'd forgotten her promise to Chloe. But they had come cross-country to Lyndon Point to look for a home with room for the quilt shop, not necessarily to while away their time on the shores of Puget Sound. Time enough for that after they settled in. Besides, Edna already had gone to the trouble of arranging the tour. Lucie almost groaned out loud.

Fair was fair, though. She'd have to apologize and promise her daughter something in exchange for the delay to their walk on the beach.

Lucie launched negotiations as soon as they stepped out of the diner, and Chloe kept them up as they drove behind Edna's cherry-red convertible to the cottage at the other end of town.

Although Lucie was certain the large, ratty-looking Victorian was the place for her, she couldn't stop the spurt of excitement when she parked by the gate in the white picket fence. Was she about to tour her new home?

Chapter Three

A while later, Lucie cast the cottage a final look. "It's not the one, Edna. But you were right. It is an adorable house with amazing views of the sound. Who wouldn't like to live in such a sweet place? I did hope it would work for us, but it's too small for our needs."

Edna latched the gate and joined Lucie and Chloe on the sidewalk. "So did I, dear. So did I." She jiggled the keys she'd used to open the lockbox. "When you emailed me your requirements, right away I imagined pretty quilts and all kinds of colored fabrics in the different rooms of an old, historical home. Don't you think this one would make the nicest little shop, even if not yours?"

Lucie unlocked her rental car. "That's what I thought when I first saw it on the internet. When you showed me the printouts at the diner, I agreed it had potential. But now that the tape measure has given its verdict, I realize it's not for me. To begin with, I have to set up a quilting frame and still fit students around it to teach stitching techniques. This house doesn't have a single room with that kind of space."

It was Edna's turn to sigh. "Oh, I know, I know. I understand what you need much better now. It's too bad. This is a wonderful house and we don't have many historical properties on the market right now."

A tug on Lucie's sundress wiped away all thoughts of her store. And the perfect Victorian. Before she turned to Edna again, she gestured with an upright index finger for Chloe to give her one more minute.

"What's worse about this sweet dollhouse," Lucie added, "is that it doesn't offer us living space. Chloe and I need at least a couple of rooms for ourselves." She faced her daughter. "What's up?"

The five-year-old shoved her pink hat brim out of the way and squinted against the sunshine. "When do we go to the beach, Mama? Is it time now?"

It had taken United Nations–worthy bargaining to get them to the house without a major meltdown. Now, it was time to pay up.

Lucie smiled. "You've been so patient, peanut. How about we go now? Hop in."

Once she had Chloe buckled, Lucie closed the door and faced her Realtor again. "I meant what I said at lunch. I know the big Victorian is the right place. Please look into it for me. It's clear the owner doesn't care if it falls down, but I would love to bring it back to life."

Edna wouldn't meet Lucie's gaze. She made a vague noise and fussed with the zipper of her briefcase.

What was the deal with the Victorian? What made Edna so uncomfortable?

One way or another, Lucie was going to find out. She pushed some more. "It's a shame to have such a run-down structure in the middle of a beautiful downtown. I did a lot of research before I put the town at the top of my list of potential places to raise Chloe. Everything I've seen about Lyndon Point so far only reinforces my initial feelings."

Lyndon Point was the right place for her and Chloe.

Especially since her daughter's father lived here. Now that Lucie had found Ryder, father and daughter should be able to establish a close relationship. And she would do everything she could to encourage it.

As long as Ryder proved to be the kind of father Chloe deserved.

Even if tonight's dinner promised to be difficult and emotionally draining, Lucie had to do the right thing. The responsible thing. The mature thing.

She'd known introducing Ryder and their daughter would be hard. How could it not be? The guy hadn't had a clue about the child's existence. Sure, he was going to be mad. And stunned. And who knew what other reactions he might come up with.

If nothing else, she would learn a lot about the kind of man he was by how he handled the news.

She'd deal with the rest of the town's reaction after she scaled that emotional mountain. Because she would have to. The townspeople were bound to be curious. And form opinions.

What *were* they going to say? Would they think Ryder had abandoned his child? Kept her a secret all those years? That might make them think he was a total rat.

Lucie's stomach lurched. "Whoa…" She couldn't do that to him.

Oh, Father God, I need Your strength. Chloe…Ryder… his family—

"Are you okay?" Edna asked.

"F-fine."

Lucie had no idea when she'd be okay again. But it wasn't the time to focus on that. She'd have to face it soon enough.

At dinner.

When she told Ryder.

At that moment, however, Lucie had to focus on her business future—her quilt shop. She still had a daughter to support. And a thing or two to prove to her overprotective father and brothers back home, doubters all three.

She went on. "I like everything I've seen in Lyndon Point, except maybe the condition of that poor house. It needs help. And I know I'm the one to give it the love and care—the help—it needs."

"I'm so glad you appreciate our town," Edna said, grasping at a topic she seemed to like better. "And if you want to get a true feel for life in Lyndon Point, Birdie's Nest, the diner where we had lunch, is the place to go. Everyone in town pops in at least once or twice a week. If anything's happened since you last stopped by, you'll learn all about it the minute you walk into the Nest."

Lucie frowned. "I'm not so sure I'm up for a gossip pit."

Edna laughed. "That's the last thing I'd call the Nest. But you're a big-city girl, aren't you?"

"Guilty as charged. I grew up in Connecticut, and Hartford's pretty big. After high school, I went to college in Houston—everything's huge in Texas. Then, for six years—up until three weeks ago—I worked in New York. 'Nuff said."

The stately Edna hitched up the shoulder strap of her briefcase and smoothed her tailored slate silk tunic over her hips. She checked her reflection in the driver's side window of Lucie's rental car. Satisfied, she turned back to Lucie.

"Another appointment," she explained. "Anyway, you're in for a treat in Lyndon Point, dear. You couldn't get me to live in a big city for all the chocolate in the world. Nobody knows you, nobody cares and you don't know who you can count on when you really need a hand…or a hug."

Lucie couldn't keep the skepticism out of her voice. "And this Birdie's Nest provides all that?"

"No, honey. No diner can provide those things. Only a tight-knit community can do that. Lyndon Point is nothing if not tight-knit. But that's not something you'll 'get' by talking to me. You'll get it once you've lived here awhile."

"Fair enough—"

"Ma-*maaaaa!*"

Lucie smiled. "How about you tell me the shortest way to the nearest strip of beach?"

Moments later, armed with Edna's directions scribbled on the back of her business card, Lucie drove away from the cottage and through the bustling, if small and quaint, downtown.

Main Street, a curving road lined with beautiful Victorians and vintage Western bungalows, most of which had been turned into businesses, looked like something out of a postcard. A handful of attractive two- and three-story buildings from the twenties and thirties were tucked in among the houses, and the mix made for an appealing commercial corridor. Lucie smiled, more certain by the minute that this was the right place for her and Chloe. For more reasons than just Ryder.

Lyndon Point felt right. Had Ryder not been there, it would have felt the same. Lucie had done her homework before selling her car, and packing up or selling off everything in her condo before putting it up for sale. After the closing, she booked the flight west for her and Chloe, leaving the rest of their belongings in storage, ready to follow once they found a place to put them. But until she'd driven through town this second time, she hadn't realized how good a job she'd done on her research.

Besides a father for Chloe, Lucie wanted a different

lifestyle more than anything else, one that gave her and Chloe more time together. She also wanted the chance to pursue her dream: her own quilt and needle arts shop. She'd studied fashion and textile design in college, and six years had given her more than her fill of the fashion world. But she'd never lost her love for the tactile pleasure of running quality fabric through her hands. She especially loved the works of art one could make from bits and pieces of those delicious textiles.

"Oh, wow!" She slowed down as she eased onto the street Edna had indicated.

"Would you look at that, Chloe-girl?" She couldn't tear her gaze away from the amazing view. The sky stretched out forever, a fresh-washed, faded-denim expanse. Not a cloud marred the endless blue. Along the street, immeasurably tall evergreens curtained the homes and cast shadows over the car. At the end of the street, the cul-de-sac hemmed the rocky beach, visible behind the last house. The waters of the mystical Puget Sound lapped the rocks.

In the distance, the horizon glowed as a shadowy seam that blurred the end of the sound and the start of the sky. Off to a side, the dark silhouette of one or another of the San Juan Islands drew her attention to its mysterious allure. Lucie drank deep of one of the most spectacular sights she'd ever come across.

Awed by the magnificence of God's creation, she whispered, "Thank You, Jesus."

She took hope. The God who'd made such beauty could surely repair the unintended mess she and Ryder had made of their lives, and Chloe's, nearly six years ago.

She again placed her hope in that God.

At five o'clock that evening, Ryder walked out of his office, his thoughts miles away.

"Did you call your aunt Myra?" Wendy asked.

"Wha—yes!" He had to get a grip. He hadn't survived dinner with Lucie yet, and he'd never get the answers he wanted if he spent their time together all zoned out.

With a deliberately long-suffering smile, he said, "Yes, Wendy. I called Aunt Myra."

She gave him a steady stare over her glasses. "And did you cave?"

"Of course I didn't cave."

"Humph!" She rose to her full five-foot height. "Let me rephrase that, Boss. Are you going to bail her out again?"

They'd had this discussion many times before. Ryder didn't want to waste energy on it, but once again Wendy wasn't about to cut him any slack. She stared him down.

"I'm not bailing her out," he said. "I'm going to look over the books, check into what last quarter's interest income for the family trust looks like and see what I can come up with to help."

Wendy closed her desk drawer with a hip. "You're bailing her out, Ryder. Like you do all the time."

"No, I'm troubleshooting. She has a financial problem. I'm an accountant and the executor of the family trust. I can help."

As she snagged a full water bottle with one hand, Wendy crammed her yellow bike helmet on her head with the other. On her way to the door, she gave him one of her too-wise looks over her shoulder. "Think about it, Boss. What would happen if you let her thrash around on her own?"

When he wouldn't answer, she went on. "Myra would be forced to figure out a way to make her business profitable, wouldn't she? And if she couldn't cut it without you propping her up, she'd go under. If that's the case, should she be in business in the first place? That's what you tell your other clients. Why not her?"

The only problem with a brilliant, efficient and truly likable if pushy and all-too-knowing assistant was that Ryder had no real desire to fire her. Even at those times when she drove him nuts. Like now.

"Aunt Myra has money," he said. "A share of the interest from the trust belongs to her, and if she wants to invest it in her business, I'll help her do it. This is different from those other clients' situations."

Wendy rolled her eyes. "Yep. Like I've said a bunch of times before, she's one of your relatives. Myra knows she can play you like a banjo, so she does. And you cave. You've got a thing for being *the* hero to everyone around here."

Before he could argue any further, Wendy walked away, leaving him to stare after her through the office's wide front window. She spun the combination on her bike's lock, jumped on and raced away, muttering the whole time. He was glad he couldn't hear.

This wasn't the first time they'd had that argument, if not in particular about Aunt Myra. Wendy insisted Ryder had some weird kind of need to be…well, needed by his numerous extended family members.

But that wasn't right. He simply had a large family, on both sides, and many of them were problem-prone. Ryder was good at problem solving. It was why he'd been elected mayor. Problem solving was what he did best.

And now, he really was going to have to put his problem-solving talents to especially good use. On his own behalf.

What was he going to say to Lucie at dinner? He'd rather eat worms than come across like a lovesick fool.

Still…why *had* she come to Lyndon Point? There was

no way he was going to buy any babble about its homey, small-town appeal. The good ole U.S. of A. had more of those places than any one person could live long enough to count. Or check out.

If he remembered correctly, she'd said something about him playing a part in her decision. He wasn't so vain as to think she'd tracked him down to reignite their summer romance.

His stomach kicked up a little hitch, but he tamped down the reaction to that crazy thought. As attractive as Lucie was, and as incapable as he was to ignore the attraction he felt, he knew he couldn't make the same mistake again. Wasn't gonna happen. The woman hadn't bothered to come after him. It had been a very long time. He must not have meant as much to her as she had to him.

But what if…?

What if in the normal course of day-to-day life they found that the old feelings hadn't died? Was he ready for the chance to find out what a future with Lucie might hold?

The possibility sent him reeling. It boggled the mind.

"Lord?" he whispered. "Is that why You let this happen?"

For them to even have a chance, she was going to have to answer a truckload of questions. Like, why? Why had she kept her name, her complete identity, from him? What had made her so secretive back then?

Did she have something horrible to hide?

And if, as she'd said, he was part of her reason to choose Lyndon Point, had it *really* taken her six years to find him?

What was Lucinda Adams hiding?

Because, as well as he knew his own name, Ryder knew Lucie was keeping something from him.

Ryder rubbed his eyes with the heels of his hands. What was he going to do about Lucie? She had taken over every last one of his thoughts.

Again.

Lucie arrived at the diner fifteen minutes ahead of their agreed-upon time. She'd known she would need to gather her thoughts and tamp down her emotions before she faced Ryder again. She wanted to start the evening with at least an outward show of maturity.

Chloe hadn't wanted to stay behind at the hotel with the grandmotherly babysitter Lucie had interviewed earlier that afternoon, so she'd had to deal with that skirmish already. While up to now she'd never left her daughter with someone she barely knew, Lucie couldn't have tonight's conversation with Ryder while their daughter was anywhere nearby.

Still, she didn't look forward to doing battle again today.

With a mental tug at her determination, Lucie locked the rental car and walked down the sidewalk toward the front of the diner. She couldn't stop wondering how Ryder would respond to her this time. She also had qualms about her reaction to him.

Especially when it came to Chloe.

Still, the extreme awareness she experienced in Ryder's presence was undeniable. His appeal remained as strong as ever.

But tonight wasn't about her. Tonight was about Chloe.

Lucie was used to making all the decisions that affected her daughter. As soon as she told Ryder the truth, she would have to surrender part of that duty…that privilege. Which didn't sit too well with her.

Chloe was *her* daughter. From fighting her father when

he'd suggested Lucie opt for an abortion or at the very least adoption, to choosing Chloe's pediatrician, her preschool, even the socks she wore each day, Lucie had shouldered all responsibility for the child she loved more than anything. She'd done it for Chloe and had relished every minute of it. She still did.

But Chloe had two parents. Now that Lucie had found Ryder again, he had a right to share in their daughter's up-bringing. And Lucie was going to have to let him partici-pate in future decisions.

Whether she liked it or not.

She'd battled her father and two older brothers to keep decision making in her hands. She'd known they meant well, but the Adams men were true control freaks. Since Lucie was the youngest child and the only daughter, she had borne the full force of their heavy-handed, misguided efforts to manage her life, especially after she'd come back from college pregnant. They always said—even now, at her age of twenty-eight—that they wanted to help her avoid another monumental mistake, that they wanted to protect her and keep her moving in the right direction. She'd felt smothered.

Early in her pregnancy, Lucie decided not to let the guys run her baby's life, and for the most part, she'd kept it that way over the years. But they'd never let up pushing their advice on her, even when they should have known their latest suggestion was the furthest thing she'd want for her-self or her little girl. Their rules, regulations and expecta-tions finally reached the point where she hadn't been able to stomach them anymore. That had been another reason for her move west.

Finding Ryder's picture on the Lyndon Point web-site, identifying him as the town's much respected new mayor, had of course been the far more important reason.

Regardless of the state of Lucie's heart, Chloe and Ryder deserved to know each other.

Too bad she hadn't found him years ago. She had tried so hard…she'd even sought out a private investigator.

It was almost anticlimactic to find Ryder at the time when she'd been looking for a fresh start. Because of him and his long-ago mention of the Pacific Northwest, she'd focused her search on the region when she'd looked for small towns with thriving business communities. She supposed, in some vague, naive way, she'd hoped to find him again someday, hoped a search while she was actually in the area would get better results.

Maybe.

Or maybe Chloe's increasing questions about her daddy had pushed Lucie more than she'd realized.

Now they were meeting for dinner.

When she rounded the corner of the diner, she saw Ryder speaking to an older gentleman outside Birdie's Nest, back against a tree in the sidewalk, leg bent at the knee, foot propped on the trunk. He looked relaxed. He even laughed at something the other man said.

She, instead, felt nervous, anxious and uncertain.

Should she tell him tonight? Was she ready? Did she know for absolutely sure she could trust him?

There was also the issue of how she should tell him. Should she lead up to it carefully or should she simply spit it out?

Shouldn't she first see how he felt about children? What he thought about their child? True, he'd only met Chloe a few hours ago, and only for a few moments.

How would he take the news?

More importantly, was she ready to trust him with her child?

Chapter Four

As panic threatened to overtake Lucie, Ryder saw her. When his blue-gray gaze met hers—so like Chloe's—the impact shook her.

How many times had those eyes looked at her with tenderness? How many times in that crazy week had the intensity of his gaze stirred up emotions she'd never known before...or since? How many times had she looked into their cool depths, hoping to see feelings similar to hers—

"Are you ready?"

Ryder's rich voice flowed over her like it did in the memories she'd treasured for years. But this wasn't the time for memories. It was time for dinner. And talk.

She dipped her head. "Of course."

"Would you like me to drive? Or do you want to follow me?"

She hadn't expected that. Hmm...the inside of a car offered close quarters. She wasn't ready for so much togetherness. Not yet. "Where are we going? I thought we were eating here."

He grinned. "Not unless you want everyone in Lyndon

Point to visit their chiropractor tomorrow from craning their necks to listen and watch us."

She arched a brow. "And Edna insisted the diner's not a gossip pit."

"Edna?"

"Yes. Edna Lyndon is my Realtor. She's helping me look for a home."

"I see." He cleared his throat. "Anyway, the Nest is not a gossip pit. Not really. But it is everybody's favorite gathering spot, and they all know me. If they see me with a woman they don't know, they'll be curious."

Especially if the curious are females on the hunt.

Lucie had to bite her tongue to keep from blurting out the retort. Ryder really was a great-looking man. And he wasn't taken.

When she didn't answer, he shrugged, as if strangers wanting to know all about his private life were no big deal. Lucie supposed it wasn't. For him.

"Where do you suggest we eat?" she asked.

"There's a great restaurant with tall, private booths in Edmonds. It's not too far away, about a ten-minute drive closer to Seattle than we are. I can vouch for their food."

"Okay." Her nerves stretched tighter by the minute. She didn't care where they went. She doubted she'd taste a bite of her meal. "I'd better follow you." At his frown, she added, "I have to get to know the area. I am moving here, remember?"

Ryder looked as though he wanted to argue, but instead he compressed his lips, squared his shoulders, then nodded and started toward the diner's parking lot. "I think you'll like this place."

The surreal quality of the moment struck Lucie. They were speaking like strangers, as though they'd met a short time ago and were going on their first date. Through the prism of time and hard-earned insight, she realized they hadn't known each other six years ago, either.

A lot of time had gone by since they first met. They weren't the same people who'd splashed and laughed and loved on that sandy beach. Now, they had to start again.

With a child hanging in the balance.

An hour and a half later, Ryder decided that if Lucie made one more ultra-polite comment, he was going to choke.

They'd been doing an irritating verbal dance since they'd sat in the deep booth at *e-pu-lo,* the restaurant in Edmonds. Nothing about the woman on the other side of the table seemed familiar. Other than maybe her facial features. And even those looked somehow different.

In Baja, she'd been lightly tanned and she'd worn her wavy hair long and loose. Now, her fair skin looked like porcelain, while she tied her honey-colored hair into a sleek knot at the base of her neck. He assumed this style was more convenient for a working mother, but he was sure the gold-shot silk lengths would look much better if she let them flow and catch the light.

Her eyes…well, those were the same, a warm green polished with sparkles of gold. Main difference was that they didn't meet his gaze now. On the rare occasion when they almost did, he thought he'd spotted a strange emotion in them, maybe anger or accusation.

But how could that be? She was the one who'd run off to her regular life while he'd stayed on that hot, lonely beach, staring after her, wishing she'd given him the slightest encouragement to make more of their relationship.

He supposed their situation was awkward for her, too. Which led to his burning question. And he wasn't willing to give her any more time—their waiter had brought dessert ten minutes ago. No more time, not even if she had half her molten chocolate cake à la mode still sitting and melting on her plate.

"Why Lyndon Point?" he asked, his gaze glued to her face. He didn't want to miss even the faintest twitch of expression. "And don't give me a list of all its finer points. I know them well."

Slowly, she took a sip of water, replaced the glass on the table and finally met his gaze. "Because you're here."

He wasn't sure how to take her response. "You can't really think we're about to take up where we left off. Not when you walked away without sparing another thought for the fool you left standing on that beach."

There! That hint of anger. It flashed in and out of her eyes again. Was it…blame, maybe? That didn't make sense. How could she blame him for any of what had happened?

The flicker of whatever had blazed over and out of her features so fast that Ryder couldn't be sure he'd really seen it. And he didn't get a chance to ask about it, either.

Lucie gave a humorless chuckle. "Trust me, I spent a whole lot of time and energy thinking of you."

She set down her spoon, uneaten chocolate cake on it, dabbed her mouth with her napkin, folded the linen square and tucked it under the lip of her plate. She took a deep breath before going on. "A short time later, after graduation, I returned to Baja, but no one at any hotel, motel or rooming house in the area knew a guy named Ryder. Now I know why." A touch of sarcasm twisted her features.

"Is that it? That's your explanation?"

As she seemed to search for an answer, brow furrowed in thought, Ryder's frustration took over. "Something's missing from this picture. How about you tell me the reason for your sudden appearance in Lyndon Point?

I don't know where to start to glue what you've told me into something that makes sense or tells me what you're up to—"

"My goodness, Antonio!" a woman called out. "Look who's here tonight, too."

The familiar female voice, spiced with the essence of Italy, broke into Ryder's train of thought. He stood to greet the couple who'd approached the table.

He hugged the lovely middle-aged lady, and had both cheeks kissed. He held a hand out to the man. "Mrs. Carlini, Mr. Carlini. How nice to see you both!"

"And who would your beautiful companion be?" Mr. Carlini asked.

Resigned now to the gossip that would buzz through the Nest in the morning, Ryder stepped aside to help Lucie stand, and made the introductions. "She's a newcomer to Lyndon Point." To his dinner date, he added, "Mr. and Mrs. Carlini are the owners of the best pizza parlor anywhere near Lyndon Point. I know you're going to love their pies."

Lucie smiled, spoke the right words, but Ryder could tell she was not quite in the moment. The Carlinis, however, had both their antennae perked and ready to capture whatever vibes he and Lucie sent out. A dangerous situation, since Marianna Carlini, a distant cousin of his late mother, was Aunt Edna's closest friend.

"Tell me, dear," she said to Lucie, "what is your plan to do in our little town?"

"I'm going to open a quilt shop...." Lucie went into a good amount of detail, which told Ryder she might actually have thought through the tough realities in budding entrepreneurship.

"Surely a beauty like you isn't unspoken for yet," Mr. Carlini said.

At Lucie's surprising denial of any romantic relationship, Mr. Carlini continued. "*Bene, bene!* Our boy Ryder here is…what you say? Skittish about romance, too. Or is that for horses, that word?"

Lucie slanted Ryder a questioning glance, but he chose to answer Mr. Carlini's query rather than what hovered in her gaze. "It works either way, for people or horses, it's the same. But I'm not skittish. I've been busy with work, my campaign for mayor and now, actually running things. Besides, I haven't found the right woman yet." He turned to Mrs. Carlini, winked at her. "You are one in a million, Mrs. Carlini. And taken already—my loss."

Mrs. Carlini blushed. "Ah…Ryder. That won't work with me. I know you. Even our Gabriella say you're once bitten, twice shy. I ask Edna what that means, and she say Gabriella thinks you had bad luck in love once, maybe twice."

Ryder felt the last of his composure fly right out the restaurant's door. Aunt Edna, his favorite relative, surrounded herself with women very much like her. She'd said any number of times she wouldn't rest until she saw him well and wed. Mrs. Carlini had to be diverted from pursuing one of the ladies' favorite pastimes, plotting his marital prospects.

"Is Gabi back?" he asked, hoping to change the subject.

Mrs. Carlini's cheer sagged, and Ryder felt rotten.

"No," she answered, then sighed. "Not yet. But soon, she says. She's promised a long vacation here at home soon."

Ryder and Gabi Carlini had gone through school together, though their friendship had lessened after they'd chosen different coasts for school. He had gone to San Diego State, while she went to Virginia Tech for a brief time before transferring somewhere in the Midwest.

"Well, let her know she's missed around here. And she'd better pay up that Garbage Special she owes me."

His favorite pizza at Tony's, the Carlinis' place, was a decadent construction coated with a blanket of each of the countless toppings they offered. To eat at Tony's meant one had to park all thought of cholesterol and calories at the door and go for the ultimate taste experience. And tons of leftovers. The Carlinis never skimped.

"You don't need Gabi for that." Mr. Carlini patted Ryder on the back. "You come to Tony's anytime you want. Eat… what you say? Off my dime. Right?"

Mrs. Carlini cooed. No other way to describe it. He'd heard it—she'd cooed. A glance her way set off Ryder's self-preservation alarm. Still, she beat him to the punch.

"I know!" she said, her dark eyes snapping with mischief. "You bring her—" Mrs. Carlini pointed at his dinner companion "—your lovely Lucie. You bring her when you come. We'll show her a proper welcome to Lyndon Point."

He winced. Watched Lucie shrink deeper into the booth.

Mrs. Carlini turned to Lucie. "What's better than the perfect pizza to celebrate your move to town? And in our handsome mayor's company, too."

"Oh, I'm afraid the move's going to take all my time—"

"You're mistaken, Mrs. Carlini. She's not *my* lovely Lucie—"

"No, no, no!" Mrs. Carlini was on a roll and she wasn't about to be derailed. "It's a perfect plan—it's come together, no? We got to love it. Is not that what people say?"

Lucie shot Ryder a glare. "There's my little girl—"

He scowled right back. "They don't have a house yet—"

Both fell silent. Ryder stared anywhere but at her. Out the corner of his eye he saw Lucie study her used napkin. "We were finishing here, and it's getting late," she said. "I must get back to Chloe. She's been all this time with a hotel babysitter, someone she doesn't know well."

"Chloe?" Mrs. Carlini said. "Such a beautiful name. Who is Chloe?"

A soft smile eased the tension from Lucie's face. "My little girl. It's been a pleasure to meet you, and I will stop for pizza one of these days. I promise."

As she bent to retrieve her purse, Ryder hurried the Carlinis on their way. The last thing he'd expected that particular evening was one of Aunt Edna's cronies' matchmaking attempts. He didn't need any help. He could make a mess of his love life all by himself. As he had with Lucie, once upon a time.

When the Carlinis left, he collapsed into the booth for a moment. He couldn't imagine how Lucie felt after that fiasco. It had to have been awkward for her. He tipped his head in the direction of the older couple. "After that, you're still sure of your move out here?"

She nodded, but scooted to the edge of the booth as though to leave.

Ryder leaned toward her, unwilling to let her go. True, it was late and Chloe had been with the sitter for a while, but Lucie still hadn't given him a satisfactory explanation for her move. They weren't leaving yet.

"So, Lucie Adams," he said, curiosity raging. "Back to where we were before the Carlinis. Why Lyndon Point?"

She seemed to sag for a moment, and then she took a sip from her almost empty water glass, lowered her head and closed her eyes. In that brief moment, Ryder had the feeling she was praying. When she looked up, her eyes shone with unshed tears. "I had no choice."

Ryder grimaced as he shook his head. "What do you mean? Of course you had a choice. There's a whole country, the whole United States. You could make a home for yourself and your little girl anywhere."

This time, she swallowed hard, took a deep breath and laced her fingers together.

"You're right," she said.

"Go on."

She met his gaze with tear-damp eyes. "I had to come because—" a deep inhale "—because you're here. Chloe's yours, you know."

Chapter Five

Ryder supposed he did. Know about Chloe. Somewhere deep in his heart.

From the very start, the possibility had niggled at him, but it was one he hadn't wanted to face.

From the moment he'd seen Lucie again, when she'd said she had a child, he'd done everything he could to avoid giving the idea any credence. He hadn't wanted to consider it. Much less, accept it as true.

But thoughts of Chloe hadn't left him alone. He'd known. Cindy—*Lucie*—was not the kind who would have jumped from his bed into another man's.

Which was why he hadn't been willing to put off this conversation any longer. Still, her confirmation of his suspicions hit him hard. Hearing the words stunned him, shocked him with the magnitude of his new reality. If someone asked, he would have said the earth had shifted under his feet.

Ryder looked down only to see his fingers tremble. The shivers echoed the shudders deep inside him, set off by the uncertainty that had shattered his characteristic assurance.

He squared his shoulders and gulped some water. He

might as well settle back into the booth. There was no question. They weren't going anywhere—not now. Not until he got answers to all his questions, questions that, up until seconds ago, he hadn't realized he had.

"How about you go back to the beginning," he said. "Start in Baja. Tell me everything. And I do mean everything, *Lucie*."

She shrugged. "It's not that complicated. I already told you most of it."

"That's it? You checked out a couple of places at the beach?"

Her fingers flew in a gesture of frustration, then both hands clenched. She planted the fists on the tabletop. Leaned toward him.

"No! That's not it. I tried to weasel information from all the airlines that went anywhere near Baja. But being post-9/11, I got nowhere. I suppose you didn't fly down in the first place.... You didn't, did you?"

"I went to school in San Diego. We drove down."

Again, she arched that brow. "I also checked in with the police, and they looked at me as though they wanted guys in white coats to take me away. I even tried to get a P.I. to look for you."

She closed her eyes, paused and shook her head. "But guess what? You never told me your real name, where you were from, not even where you went to school or what you planned to do with your life. The P.I. said I didn't have enough for him to go on, so he refused, as he put it, to steal my cash."

Ryder was glad for the dim ambience at *e-pu-lo*. His cheeks blazed at her words. Yes, he had started out their romance as a vacation thing. But so had she.

He rubbed his temples, where a headache had taken root. "I already told you, too. I didn't try to mislead you.

I've always been called Ryder. That's how we were introduced. But, yeah, okay. It's not my *real* first name."

She flicked her fingers in a dismissive wave. "Fine. You didn't try to deceive me, but you weren't a fount of info, either. The results were the same. I had no way to find you. Until I saw your picture on the Lyndon Point website."

"Isn't that conveniently coincidental?"

"Are you suggesting I somehow knew all along where you were but didn't do a thing about it until now? What kind of rotten person do you think I am?"

"I don't think you're rotten—"

"Okay, fine. For the record, I didn't know where you were. Period. And every time I tried to find you—zip! No trace of Ryder. Let's face it, unless you had your picture plastered all over the web before you assumed your mayoral duties, how was I supposed to figure out where you were? And while I did keep looking for you all those years, I didn't pine away all that time, either, if that's what you're thinking."

Her anger came across in waves, and she didn't give him a chance to speak. "How about you? I haven't heard a whole lot about any efforts to find me on your part."

His turn to scoff. "Oh, sure, *Cindy*. I had lots and lots to go on." He looked down at the table, at his mostly intact strawberry shortcake. He pushed it away. "I did look for you. I tried all the motels and hotels. Airlines, too. Like you say you did. And with no more success than you."

She tilted her head, lifted a shoulder. "I'll give you that. I did have one comment you made about a family vacation in the Pacific Northwest when you were a kid. I followed that trail as much as I could, even though it led nowhere. I came right back to it this time, too. This time, it paid off."

"I told you about that trip?"

She nodded. "You said something about taking the ferry out from Seattle. But try finding Ryder in Seattle…or anywhere else. You told me it was a family vacation. You could have traveled here from anywhere."

She seemed to find something of great interest in the puddle of ice cream muddled in with the molten chocolate of her cake. When she spoke again, she did so in a quiet voice, one that revealed a hint of uncertainty and even more vulnerability.

"I suppose I always held some irrational hope of—um—looking for you again. Maybe after moving out here. And… well, you know the rest. That's how I'm here now."

Although her voice tugged at him and her expression reminded him of the last look she'd given him on the beach, Ryder steeled himself against her appeal.

Her surprisingly strong appeal.

"And Chloe?" he asked, fighting to stay focused. "What about the pregnancy? When did you know? Tell me about that."

She told him how she'd returned to Houston. How weeks later, she'd struggled with violent nausea during finals, certain she'd caught a bug in Mexico. When she could no longer deny what she'd begun to suspect, she'd gone for a pregnancy test.

She sighed. "That's when my efforts to find you kicked into high gear." Her vague wave revealed a tremor in her slender fingers. "By that point, I was sad, scared and morning sick, so I took my diploma, my hot job offer, and went back East. There I had to tell my family thanks, but no thanks for their efforts to butt in. I struck out on my own. I wanted to raise my daughter—"

She caught herself. Her eyes opened wide. She swallowed. "*Our* daughter. I wanted to raise her my way."

Their daughter. He shuddered.

Before he could ask where he came in, other than making Chloe in the first place, Lucie went on.

"I never gave up hope of finding you. For Chloe's sake."

Her words echoed in his head. *For Chloe's sake.* What about for her sake? Reason made him put the thought aside.

He rubbed his forehead, where a dull throb had set up. "Well. Looks like you found me. Now what?"

"Chloe needs a father, and you deserve to know your daughter." She again laced the fingers of both hands so tight that, even in the dim light, he saw the knuckles pale. "As soon as I realized you were here, the only thing I could do and live with myself was to come to Lyndon Point."

"You're saying you didn't stay away all those years to keep her from me."

"On the contrary." She shook her head in clear exasperation. "How many times do you want me to say it? I've told you and told you. I tried. I really did. Now it's up to you to believe me or not. The bottom line is I tried to find you, but couldn't. No conspiracy, no intrigue."

She was right. He didn't know what to believe. It all was too haphazard. He pressed the bridge of his nose between his finger and thumb. In a weird, disjointed way, his mind registered restaurant sounds and smells but they seemed to come from a great distance. Amazing how his life had narrowed to the space contained within this small booth.

To Lucie. And him.

As thoughts and emotions battled inside him, Lucie again broke the silence. "I know it makes no sense. I really did hope to bump into you someday, once I moved out here. It's crazy, sure, but there you have it. And…well, you know the rest. I really do want you to know Chloe." Lucie's smile turned gentle and warm. "She is yours."

To his surprise, a knot formed in his throat. He nodded, unwilling to embarrass himself with a croaked response. Moments went by. When he felt able to speak in a somewhat normal voice, he said, "I don't doubt you on that account. The numbers add up, and I don't think you'd lie about something this important."

"Wait until you see her minus the hat. She looks like what she is, a mix of you and me." Her breath caught. More tears brightened her eyes.

Ryder gave her a handful of moments before speaking. "Like I said before, what's next? Where do we go from here?"

"I'm not going anywhere. I've made my move—across the country. Now I'm looking for a place to live. Near Chloe's dad."

Dad. He was a dad.

"Wow," he said in a quiet, awe-filled voice. "I have a… Chloe. It's going to take me some time to get my head around the concept. But, you know? As new as all this is for me, I do want to get to know my—" he shook his head in wonder "—my daughter. I'd like to start right away."

She swallowed hard. "I figured as much. But you see…" A breath…another. She seemed to come to a decision. "I'm not sure how best to go about it. I'm no child psychologist or anything. I'm her mom. But I don't think spilling the news on her out of the blue is going to do her any good."

He narrowed his eyes. "What are you trying to say? After all this, you're going to keep me from seeing her?"

"No! Of course not. But I don't think we should show up with balloons and a marching band and say something like, 'Surprise, Chloe! Look what I found. It's a daddy!'"

Ryder had to bite down on his tongue to keep from countering her sarcasm with more of the same. He realized his reaction came from a sense of disappointment. He had a sudden urge to be just that: Chloe's daddy. But...

"You have a point," he said, his voice tight. "I hadn't thought of that." He ran a hand over his face, rubbed his eyes. "I haven't had a chance to think through anything. It's too new. First, you. Then finding out that I, Matthew Ryder Lyndon, am a father."

He shook his head in wonder. "You've got to give me leeway here. You've had six years of mommy-hood. I've had, what? Fifteen minutes? Well, not of mommy-hood. You understand."

This smile was sweet and understanding. "You'll have the rest of your life now. I'm only asking that we go carefully, to give Chloe time to get to know you. I think that's the best thing to do."

"Can we start tomorrow?"

"How about lunch?"

"I hear she's partial to barber cube sauce."

"Among other things." Lucie grinned. "But she hates peas. Most green foods are a battle."

He laughed. "Smart girl—just like her dad. I even used to pick out pieces of spices. Green stuff was evil. With age, I've evolved."

"I have a feeling you two are going to get along great."

"I sure hope so. And I'm happy to give her all the time she needs."

Their waiter returned, water pitcher in hand, but Ryder asked him for their bill. As the man walked away, he sat back in a daze. Chloe—his little girl.

A shot of pure, searing fear sliced through him. As he'd said, he hadn't thought through much of anything. What if Chloe didn't like him? What if she rejected him? What did he know about little girls?

Oh, Father in Heaven, I don't want to blow this. You're the ultimate daddy. Show me how to do right by her.

Ryder signed the credit card slip for the waiter, then helped Lucie out of the booth. As they went toward the front exit, he couldn't help but marvel at the way his day had turned. A regular, boring morning had flipped on the front steps of Birdie's Nest.

Lucie was back in his life. And she would be there for the rest of his life, thanks to Chloe.

"Any luck house hunting?" he asked. "My aunt Edna's a sharp Realtor."

"She showed me a beautiful cottage today, but it was too small for my needs."

Under the glowing streetlight, he watched her search his face as though she might find the solution to her housing problem there. She tapped her chin with an index finger, in a gesture he remembered from the past.

"You know…" she started. "As the mayor of Lyndon Point, I suppose you're familiar with the whole town."

"Not only as the mayor. I've lived there my whole life— except for college, of course."

She nodded, the wheels in her head almost visibly cranking away. "You probably know who owns which property and details like that."

He nodded, in the dark as to where this was headed.

A dazzling smile broke out across her face. "You're the one I should ask. I did see a house that would be perfect for me, but Edna insists it's not for sale." Lucie shrugged. "From what I could see, it's practically abandoned. I should be able to negotiate something with the neglectful owner."

Uh-oh. He didn't like the turn their conversation had taken. "And that house would be…?"

"I want to buy the wonderful Queen Anne Victorian

on Main Street and Sea Breeze Way. You know. The one that's practically falling down—"

"No," he said, stomach churning into knots. "Aunt Edna's right. You'd better have her find you another place. That house is *not* for sale. And it won't be. Not now, not ever."

Chapter Six

To make sure she found her way, Ryder followed Lucie back to the elegant, extended-stay hotel outside of Lynnwood, a short ten-minute drive from both Edmonds and Lyndon Point. He fumed all the way. Never in a million years would he have expected this turn of events. But maybe he should have. After all, the woman had turned his life upside down when they'd met six years ago.

Still, she wanted to buy the house? His great-great-grandfather's house? The Victorian monstrosity his younger sister, Deanna, had spent her entire life dreaming about? Talking about how she would bring it back to life, how she'd repair every last inch of it and live in it the rest of her days?

Lucie?

What about Chloe? He wasn't the most experienced man when it came to kids, but wouldn't that wreck of a place be dangerous to a little girl?

Their little girl…

First Lucie, then the revelation about Chloe and then the house. Could he envision Lucie and Chloe in Lyndon Point? Maybe. Getting to know Chloe should prove interesting. The idea of fatherhood held a certain appeal. But the house? Lucie?

No way. He couldn't see anyone in that house but Dee.

And even though Dee had vanished three years ago after an argument with Ryder, he still clung to Dee's dream. It was the only thing he had left of his sister.

He now knew he should have kept his opinion of Dee's crazy ideas under better control. He should also have realized she'd meant it when she'd said she needed to "follow her bliss," wherever that might take her. And he really should have taken seriously her relationship with Maurice, the nomadic biker who'd had little more to his name than a backpack with a clean change of clothes, tubes of oil paint, a fistful of brushes and a roll of fresh canvas—plus the motorcycle, of course. While the lifestyle of someone like Maurice inspired thoughts of anything but romance in Ryder, he should have realized an idealistic young artist like Dee would have seen Maurice as a romantic hero.

Ryder had only seen oncoming disaster for his sister. And her future.

Instead of helping prevent a tragedy, their large family had joined the fight, every last one of them taking a side. In the end, they'd contributed to the debacle. But none as much as he had. Worried sick about Dee, Ryder had argued vigorously, convinced that logic and common sense were the means to reach her, to make her face reality. He'd been wrong.

To his constant regret.

The extended family had continued to bicker, even after Dee had roared out of Lyndon Point on the back of Maurice's motorcycle. The hard feelings had lasted for months.

Worse yet, in spite of his exhaustive efforts, Ryder had

been unable to find any trace of his sister. In three years. He shuddered to think where Maurice might have taken her, what kind of life she'd been living ever since she left the safety and security of Lyndon Point and the support of their large extended family.

The most painful part was that he couldn't ignore the possibility that Dee was no longer alive. Ryder hated to go there, but reality forced him to do so. He'd found no trace of Dee, even after working with an excellent private investigator. He knew that a haphazard existence, such as the one Maurice had led, held the potential for exposure to violence.

Ryder's heart ached every time he thought of his younger sister, the sweet, creative girl his parents had always urged him to look after. But he'd failed. Miserably.

He had pushed her away, and now lived with a multitude of regrets.

Which went a long way to prove his basic philosophy. Sensible, logical, well-thought-out choices led to a stable, comfortable existence. That spelled success to him. Wild swings of spontaneity, random impulsivity, didn't.

That was one thing Dee and Lucie had in common. In the same way his sister had roared out of town on a whim, it appeared Lucie had left her life on the East Coast. True, her actions had brought him the opportunity to meet the daughter he hadn't known he had, but still, Lucie had always struck him as about as solid and steady as the butterfly with which she'd compared herself when they'd first met.

It didn't look as though she'd changed much over the years.

A sudden thought filled him with concern.

What did Lucie's impulsive, spontaneous nature bring to Chloe's upbringing? How could a woman like that raise a child without turning the child into another unpredictable adult?

Fear filled him. Even though Lucie had been raising Chloe all this time, and the little girl didn't strike him as particularly worse for the experience, could he really trust Lucie? Would she continue to mold her into another flighty, artistic female like the two who had affected the last six years of his life?

After discovering he had a daughter, was he going to risk losing Chloe like he'd lost Dee? Like he'd lost Lucie?

And how far was he willing to go to prevent it?

Lucie opened her eyes the next morning with the sense of dread from the evening before still congealed in her middle. She'd had a rough night, hadn't slept much, and what little sleep she'd found had paraded images of Ryder across her subconscious. The man was anything but sleep inducing.

"Mama…?"

Her—*their*—daughter's sleepy voice underscored why anything related to Ryder Lyndon caused serious disruption to her serenity—if she'd had any left after she'd walked away from him on that beach in Baja.

But no matter how bad an episode of insomnia he'd caused her this time, Lucie couldn't hide in the plush cocoon of her hotel bed all day. She drew a fortifying breath and stretched every inch of her body. "Mmm-hmm?"

"We going to the beach today?"

Sigh. She had promised. Again.

"Sure. We can go. But we need to get up, get dressed and eat. Mama's got to look around town to see where she's going to put her store."

Chloe sat up from her side of the king-size bed and

nodded. Her tangled honey-colored curls bounced and her gray-blue eyes took on an owlish expression. "That's right. Threads and cloths and fumbles and stuff."

"Thimbles, Chloe. They're thimbles. A fumble is something…" Something she, Lucie, had done all evening long as she'd tried to explain herself to Ryder. "Something huge men do with a football."

Another serious look and a nod. "Okay, Mama. *Fff-fimbles!*"

She'd take it. "Time to hustle, girly-girl. Shower first."

Lucie rummaged in their suitcases for something appropriate to wear. While it was early summer, the breezes off Puget Sound still bore the nip of these northern waters they'd driven so close to on their way to Lyndon Point from Seattle. By lunchtime, however, the temperature could rise enough to surprise the unwary tourist.

Even though Lyndon Point wasn't a tourist town. Maybe it should be one. Something to consider.

She wondered if Ryder, in his capacity as mayor, had plans to increase tourism, and by extension, commerce to his town. Lucie would have to start attending city government meetings now that she was going to become part of the town's business community. She wasn't sure how she felt about that. Newspapers were always full of tales of contention and woe at those events.

"Mama?"

"Yes, Chloe?"

"Ah…are we…um…can we go find me a daddy today? Kinda like we're gonna look for your *fff-fimble* store?"

"You already—" Lucie caught her bottom lip between her teeth to keep the words from bursting out. She took a shaky breath, rubbed the area where pounding had erupted at her temple and grimaced. "You don't need to go looking for a daddy, Chloe. That's not the way things work.

Keep talking to Jesus about it, okay? I'm sure He…has the answer for you."

Coward!

"Is so the way it works." The rounded chin rose up and the eyebrows met over the bridge of Chloe's nose. "You said Jesus says we have to ask so He will bless us, and I'm asking, okay? I'm asking Him to bless us with a daddy, so I'm gonna keep on looking for the daddy Jesus is gonna send us—it says so in the Bible. 'Sides, if I don't look for him, how're we gonna find him?"

The "So there!" while not voiced, rang out loud and clear in the room. Was her little girl ready for the truth? Could she wait until Ryder and Lucie prepared her? Should she have to wait?

What would be best?

Lucie sent a silent prayer heavenward. She needed her Father's guidance on this one. As the ultimate daddy, surely He would know how best to handle the situation for her daughter.

Knowing that daughter only too well, Lucie kept Chloe focused on moving through her shower. After that, she dealt with the series of controversies that arose every time Lucie tried to choose an outfit for the tiny fashionista.

A blue sundress with a hoodie on top wasn't going to cut it. Nothing but purple capri pants would do.

With Chloe dressed in the ruffly lavender tunic that matched the purple knit pants, and her curls contained by twin ponytail holders above her years, Lucie was able to persuade her daughter to watch a children's morning show while she showered and dressed.

Forty-five minutes later, the Adams women walked into the dining room at the attractive hotel. While planning the move, Lucie hadn't known how long it would take her to find the right property, so she'd chosen a long-term suite for her and Chloe. Now that she'd found her perfect house, she'd have to move somewhere else pretty soon. Her savings would cover restoring the Victorian, but wouldn't stretch far enough for an extended stay at the upscale hotel.

Filled with a greater sense of resolve, Lucie surveyed the tables in the atrium restaurant and spotted a vacant one near the lengthy buffet. She slipped her sweater and Chloe's over two of the chairs, then headed for the buffet. The white-linen-cloaked expanse groaned under the burden of massive fruit platters, baskets of rolls and pastries, chilled trays of yogurts, a colorful array of single-serving cereals and half a dozen silver chafers, from where the most mouthwatering scents arose.

"Mama?"

"Yes, Chloe?"

"Am I gonna lose my toof today? Like when I bite into breakfast?"

The tooth in question had moved only an infinitesimal bit last time Lucie had checked. "I don't think so."

Chloe's expectant smile wilted. "Oh."

Lucie led them down the buffet line, piling delicious selections on their plates. They sat, enjoyed the fresh fruits, eggs, croissants, and even Chloe fell in love with the exquisite and expensive smoked salmon Lucie offered her.

Before long, they were on their way to Lyndon Point, and Lucie was glad to find a parking spot a block down from Main Street on Sea Breeze Way. True, she'd headed there on purpose, drawn by her memory of the Victorian at the corner. As she'd approached the house, her certainty had grown stronger. She knew it was the place for her.

As the many shops opened, Lucie visited all of them, one by one. She fell in love with the women's clothing boutique, the marine-themed gift shop, the jeweler's sparkling emporia and the pine-scented stationery store, where she couldn't resist running her fingers over the display of gorgeous handmade papers.

"I'll be back," she told the owner, an older gentleman by the name of Sam Porter. "As soon as I have an address for my shop, I'll come order business cards and all my other paper needs. Your selection is impressive."

"You do that." His brown eyes twinkled behind wire-rimmed glasses. "In the meantime, here's a little something for the young lady."

To Chloe's delight, he handed her a tiny two-inch memo pad in a perfect shade of purple. Pen and Paper, the name of the store, was emblazoned in bright white across the cover. He stocked a vast collection of high-end pens right next to his magnificent paper selections, and he offered Chloe one of the plainer ones to match her memo pad.

"Thanks!" Chloe said with a grin. "I'll be back, too."

At Tea & Sympathy Lucie met Edna's friend, Shirley Wilcox. The woman was a gem, tall and slender, with a Gibson-girl knot of polished-silver hair atop her head, and brimming with a bubbly personality.

"Oh, no," she said, as soon as Lucie mentioned they'd only stopped in for a moment. "Edna told me all about you and your little girl. Now it's my turn to get to know you. Come on with me—" she waved for them to follow her toward the back of the fragrant shop "—and have a cup of tea. Take a seat. Tell me what you'd each like to try. It's on the house today, your first visit—of many, I hope."

The tea aficionada helped Lucie and Chloe choose their flavors, and after they'd finished generous cups of a light and elegant Green Earl Gray for Lucie and a sweet spiced citrus herbal Burst of Sunshine for Chloe, they headed down to the beach.

For the first time in a long time, Lucie felt a sense of

peace envelop her. True, she hadn't resolved anything yet, but she had come out to Washington State with her faith and trust firmly tucked in place at the foot of the cross. She knew bringing Chloe to meet Ryder was the right thing to do. She would trust the Father to continue to guide her through the next series of steps, whatever they turned out to be and wherever they might lead.

"Mama?"

"Yes, Chloe?"

"What's a person who collects rocks?"

"Some people call them rock hounds."

Chloe tipped her head back so she could see Lucie's face from under the bill of her purple visor, the blue-gray eyes she'd inherited from Ryder huge and questioning. "You mean like dogs? That kinda hound?"

Lucie chuckled. "The term probably comes from bloodhounds. They're the breed of dog used in search-and-rescue operations. They're pretty good at finding people. I think it means the rock hounds figure they're pretty good at finding special rocks."

Chloe accepted Lucie's explanation and wandered a few steps closer to the water.

"Watch out, honey!" Lucie called. "You don't want to get wet. We're meeting your—"

She drew in a sharp breath. She and Ryder were going to have to tell Chloe, and soon, but Lucie still felt as strongly as ever that they had to be careful, ease into the revelation, to make sure the five-year-old took the news as well as possible. Chloe was precocious, and she was going to pummel Lucie and Ryder with a barrage of questions about their situation, but she was still a little, little girl.

"Huh?" that precocious little girl asked. "Who is it we're meeting?"

"Um…well, you see…we're having lunch with someone.

He's a nice man, and he wants to get to know you. You already met him yesterday. Outside the diner."

Chloe wrinkled her nose. "You mean the guy who didn't know your name?"

Yet another pang of guilt shot through Lucie. "Yes, Chloe. That's the one."

With a shrug, Chloe bent to check out another pile of rocks. "He's kinda weird, Mama. He knows you, but he doesn't know your name—that's weird. D'ya think he'll figure mine out okay?"

Lucie doubted Ryder would ever mistake his daughter's name. His reaction to the news of her existence had been, if nothing else, positive. "I'm sure he'll do fine."

"Look, Mama!" Chloe raced back, her hands full of large, smooth beach pebbles. "These are my special ones. I'm a rock hound now, too."

Clutching her treasures, Chloe followed Lucie back up into town. As they walked down Sea Breeze Way toward the diner at the corner across from the Victorian, Lucie's fragile sense of peace began to waver. How would the lunch go? How would Ryder deal with Chloe? How would Chloe behave? How would they begin to forge the father-daughter relationship Lucie considered vital to her daughter's emotional well-being?

As they approached the corner, she found her attention again captured by the large, dilapidated house to her left. It had once been spectacular, if not a true mansion, then at least the dwelling of a pillar of the community. Someone successful enough to have the money to build a luxurious home with all the decorative trends of the time. It angered her to see such heritage decaying, dying day by day, when all it took was a little elbow grease—and a fair pile of dough—to maintain it.

"I can't believe it," she fumed, her steps growing faster.

"Would you look at that garden? I can see at least ten different rose bushes, and it looks like tulips and who knows what else hiding beneath that jungle of weeds. Why would anyone let it go like that?"

When she reached the corner, instead of heading to the diner, she crossed the street, Chloe's rock-filled hand firmly in her grasp. She stood in front of the house, *her* house. Deep inside, Lucie recognized the truth.

One way or another, with the Father's help, she would make the house hers.

Chapter Seven

Before she let herself think it through, Lucie followed her impulse and tried to open the rusty black gate. She paused for a moment to admire the loops and swirls, marveling at the talent God had given the person who'd wrought something so graceful out of—well—a lump of iron. A lump of iron that was now the lovely barrier between Lucie and the house.

Again, without taking the time to think things through, she stood on tiptoe and eased a leg over the three-foot fence. Once inside, a tall weed scratched her arm and her sandal crunched something that squished underfoot. "Oh, gross."

Ignoring the yuck factor, she yanked out the attacking weed and tossed it aside. As she'd suspected, a sunrise-orange-tipped tulip was fighting to peek out from under a shroud of smothering underbrush. Lucie yanked again and again, weed after weed, and built a small pile at her side in a minute or so.

"Whatcha doing now, Mama?"

Yank. "What someone should have been doing for the last…" Out came another weed. "Oh, I don't know…" And one more. "Maybe four or five years."

"Can I do that, too?"

Some of the weeds were taller than Chloe. But since Lucie didn't want a Chloe meltdown so close to the time they were meeting Ryder, she had to choose her words wisely. "I don't know, honey. You might get dirty, and we are going to lunch in a little while."

Still clinging to her rocks, Chloe crossed her arms and gave Lucie another stare. "How 'bout you? Aren't *you* gonna get dirty?"

"I'm being careful."

"I'll be careful, too. Promise."

Lucie sighed. "Okay, Chloe. But you have to stand right next to me, where I've cleared out some of this mess. You don't want a bug to bite you, right?"

Chloe held out her arms for Lucie to pick her up and bring her over the fence. Once she set her down again, Chloe shrugged. "You can put some more of that pink stuff on if a bug bites."

Focused on her task, Lucie returned to the plight of the golden tulip. When she vanquished a particularly lush weed, she was rewarded by the sight of a dozen or more tulips poking up through the dirt, on the verge of unfurling their velvety petals, but only if someone freed them from their cell.

That someone was Lucie. She redoubled her efforts on behalf of the golden-tulip patch.

"What do you think you're doing?" a male voice asked not ten feet away.

Lucie bolted upright and spun around, her latest leafy victim in her fist. "I'm doing what the negligent owner hasn't done." She glared at Ryder. "What's happening to this gorgeous treasure of a house is a crime. There should be a law— Wait! There is—probably more than one, I think." She brought her free hand to her brow to shelter her eyes from the bright sunlight. "Doesn't Lyndon Point have ordinances against letting a house go to ruin like this? Against creating an eyesore that devalues the surrounding properties?"

Lucie didn't quite recognize herself in the fervent gardener that had erupted, but she did recognize, way back in one of those deep, dark corners of herself, that it all stemmed from the strain caused by her situation.

By his appealing, unnerving presence.

Ryder still had the same power to affect her that he'd had in Baja six years ago. And it hadn't been just his good looks that had drawn her to him. His intelligence had challenged her. His sense of humor unarmed her. She feared it might happen again. But she couldn't let it. It had all been one-sided, and that had led to indescribable pain. She had to focus on what really mattered: Chloe and the business venture before her.

As he continued to gape at her, some foreign urge compelled her to march up to the fence before him, ignoring the weeds in her way.

"Really, Ryder. *You* of all people should know—" she shook her specimen scant inches from his face "—after all, you're the mayor. Do something. Cite the owner for… for…" She waved the weed at the house. "Aggravated architectural homicide."

Having run out of steam, Lucie dropped her arm to her side, the offending vegetation still in her clutches. Ryder no longer gaped. He'd crossed his arms in a gesture identical to Chloe's, and his mouth now made a tight, uncompromising line. His jaw looked more like it had been carved from one of Chloe's beach pebbles than from flesh and bone. Lucie was glad he'd worn sunglasses that day. She didn't want to see whatever his eyes might reveal at that moment.

"Finished?" he asked, his voice none too friendly.

"With my weed-inspired tirade?"

He nodded.

"I'm done."

"Good—"

"But not with the weeds." Lucie glanced at her watch. It was only a quarter to twelve, and they'd agreed to meet at noon. "I have fifteen minutes before I'm supposed to meet you at the diner, and I'm going to invest those fifteen minutes in clearing out some of this mess."

"You realize you're trespassing, right?"

"So who's the owner? I'll ask permission. It's obvious they don't care about the place. I doubt they'll care that I've improved its condition."

He stared from behind the sunglasses, shoulders tight, jaw tight, lips tight.

"Come on, Ryder. Who owns this place? Edna wouldn't tell me, and I doubt it's some kind of classified national-security secret."

"Secret…" He drew out the two syllables. "Now, there's a word for you."

Another pang of guilt stabbed her. She bit down on her tongue to keep from defending herself yet again. "Fine. Don't tell me. I'll get back to work and wait for you to call the cops on me. For the heinous crime of cleaning up an eyesore in the middle of town."

Lucie turned back to the tulip patch. Only then did she notice Chloe attuned to the argument. An argument Lucie had carried on mostly by herself, if she was honest. Ryder hadn't participated much.

She rose from her crouching position, turned slowly to face the father of her child, a child who'd witnessed Lucie's manic meltdown.

Her cheeks began a slow sizzle. "Ah…I'm sorry, Ryder. I can't believe I laid into you like that. Please forgive me."

That rocked the tightness in the man a bit out of whack. He slid his arms free and let them hang at his sides. His eyebrows arched over the dark upper rim of his sunglasses. A muscle twitched in the cheek that moments earlier had resembled ocean-honed rock.

"Yeah," he said. "I—it's fine. It's okay. Why don't you hop out of there so we can go eat?"

Lucie shook her head. "I said I was sorry I had a meltdown. I didn't say I was sorry for doing the right thing. I'm going to pull weeds until our agreed-upon time for lunch."

"Which is fast approaching."

She shrugged. "No problem. I'll clean now, eat in a little while and return to the weeds later. There'll be plenty of them waiting for me—if not a fresh crop of new ones that'll zoom out of the ground, now that they can see the sun."

"Mama?"

Lucie drew a fortifying breath. "Yes, Chloe?"

"He's the weird man who doesn't know your name, right? He looks like a bug with the glasses on."

She heard Ryder's sharp inhale. How was she going to maneuver her way through *this* particular minefield?

Before she could answer, however, Ryder's long legs easily cleared the iron hurdle, and he joined her and Chloe on the inside. He dropped down, placed one knee on the ground, brought his face to Chloe's level.

He removed the glasses, and to Lucie's relief, donned a smile as he studied his child. "I'm not really that weird, Chloe. Your mama…" He glanced at Lucie, squinting against the sun. "Your mama confused me with her name when we *first* met. But you helped me yesterday. You told me what her name really is."

Chloe shoved her visor back away from her forehead and stared at Ryder. Lucie sucked in a breath at the mirror images father and daughter presented. There could be no doubt who'd fathered her child.

Ryder's expression told her he knew it, too.

"Are you gonna know my name?" Chloe asked, unaware of the emotional currents around them.

Ryder extended a large hand toward her, and Lucie noticed the ghost of a tremble, quickly controlled, in the long fingers. He placed that hand on Chloe's shoulder, tentative, waiting for her response. When she didn't react, he swallowed hard, his eyes wide with what seemed to Lucie a fair dose of wonder, and finally smiled again.

"I can promise you I'll never confuse you with anyone else. Not you, not your name."

Chloe pulled out the ruffled hem of her tunic top to create a cradle for her fistfuls of ocean pebbles, then hugged the bundle close with one arm. She raised her empty hand, a finger crooked upright. "Pinky promise?"

A large, masculine digit hooked the smaller one. "Pinky promise."

This! This was why she'd moved across the country. Lucie's heart filled to overflowing. To hide her tears, she resumed her gardening, growing her stack of debris by the second.

She felt rather than saw Ryder stand and look down at her. "You're serious about the garden, aren't you?"

Over her shoulder, Lucie shot him a glance. "As serious as I can be."

She tugged, pulled, yanked and with a grunt that underscored her determination, wrested another weed from the soil.

While still hugging her rock collection, Chloe squatted next to Lucie, sent Ryder a glance over her shoulder. "I'm gonna help." With her free hand, she tore a leaf from a bushy something-or-other that hovered over the graceful tulips Lucie had unearthed and dropped it on the growing pile.

Ryder sighed. Loudly. "I guess there's only one thing for me to do."

Lucie held her breath, waiting for the phone call that would bring the town's police force after her. And Chloe. She supposed "contributing to the delinquency of a minor" would be tacked on to her other crimes.

To her surprise, Ryder's hand reached around her and grasped the woody stalk of her newest adversary. "Let me. That one's going to have deep roots."

He proceeded to yank and tug and add to Lucie's collection of detritus. And to her sudden, intense relief.

Moments later, he sent her a questioning look. "Were you a gardener in your previous, pre–Lyndon Point life?"

Remembering her office in the concrete high-rise in Manhattan, Lucie laughed so hard she fell back onto a thatch of springy, moist weeds. "Not hardly."

He loosened his royal-blue rep tie, pulled it all the way out and stuffed it in his shirt pocket. "You know, I still have no idea where you came from, other than the East Coast. That's pretty obvious. But I don't know what you do, who you really are."

She gathered her composure and rose up onto her knees again. "You're right. I never told you much about me that week."

"No, you didn't. And just so you know, I stood there on that beach like an idiot, feeling like I'd been kicked in the gut when you left. I tried to find you, but…I suppose you know how far I got looking for Cindy with honey hair and green-amber eyes."

An endless moment crawled by. She glanced toward Chloe, a few feet away, at least far enough that if Lucie and Ryder kept their tone of voice amicable, they could speak in relative privacy. "I'm from Connecticut," she said. "Hartford. That's where I grew up, where my family's from."

Ryder let out a low whistle. "You're a long way from home."

She shrugged. "I needed the change. And Chloe needs her dad."

Her word sent a visible ripple through him, made him shift his balance a notch or two. His eyes widened. "Dad…" he murmured. "I'm someone's dad—Chloe's dad." He seemed to try the concept on for size. "I'd better get used to it, huh? And I'd better be quick about it."

"Something like that." She looked around, took in the blue sky, the thriving greenery, the bustle of traffic a few feet away. Glanced at the man at her side, the child not far from him.

Uncomfortable? Sure. Still, everything felt right. Finally. "Like I told you, I do have plans—business plans. And I needed a change."

"A change? I understand a business plan, but isn't it going to be tough to adjust? Connecticut to Washington State's kind of an extreme culture shock, don't you think?"

"I wasn't living in Connecticut." A sprig of vegetation tickled her nose. She wriggled it, swiped pollen onto the shoulder of her coral knit top. "Now I'm going to paint myself like a cliché. I've been working and living in New York since college."

"New York?" He stared. "As in the Big Apple?"

"Doesn't get any bigger. I did need a change of career,

though." She held up her grubby index finger to stop him. "Before you ask…I was a fashion buyer for the last six years. I have a degree in fashion and textile design."

More questions deepened the crinkles at the corners of his eyes. But he waited for her.

She wiped a mist of sweat from her forehead with the back of her wrist. "I burned out. I've had it with the craziness of the fashion world. I want to do something else, something more meaningful—to me."

"Hmm…most women would practically kill to work in that world. And you left it like—" he snapped green-tinged fingers "—that?"

"Just like that." She went on. "I didn't get to spend as much time with Chloe as we both wanted. That was my second greatest motivator. And in the third place, I've always dreamed of opening my own shop. I'm going to give it a try."

"The economy's not in a red-hot blaze these days," he said. "Tell me, and this time with more detail than you gave the Carlinis, about that shop you want to open."

"It's a quilt and fabric store, with yarns, needlepoint and embroidery supplies, too."

He gave her answer some thought as he turned to watch Chloe deforest another shrub. "I'm sure you've thought it through." He dragged his attention back to Lucie. "But in case you need—er—*want* help, I'm an accountant by trade, and have my own firm. It's down a few blocks on Main Street."

She arched a brow. "A busy man. Running the town and keeping its accounts in order, too. It must take up a fair chunk of your time."

"Not so much that I won't be able to devote myself to Chloe."

"I wasn't implying that."

"Didn't want even the thought to cross your mind."

She blushed. The thought *had* crossed her mind. But she wasn't about to admit it. Not until she saw how he spent his time from that day forward.

A car honked as it pulled to a stop at the curb. "Hey, you three!" Edna called. "What are you doing in the middle of that mess?"

Ryder frowned. "Great."

"Cleaning up what the lazy owner won't," Lucie shouted back over the traffic noise.

"Owner's not lazy," Ryder hissed.

Lucie arched a brow, pointed to the vanquished vegetation and glared at the secretive mayor. "I'm going to shame him into selling the place to me. No matter who he hides behind."

Edna shoved her red plastic-rimmed sunglasses up on her head. She stared at Lucie, at Chloe and finally at Ryder. As she laughed and shook her head, she turned her gray eyes back to Lucie.

"You do that." She shoved the glasses back down. "I'll be on my way now." When the traffic cleared, as she started to roll again, she added, a smug smile on her lips, "You three make a *wonderful* trio. The perfect little... team!"

She knew.

At that moment, Lucie realized Edna had known from the first time they'd met. She was sure the older woman had a million questions about the circumstances that had led to the current situation. But she'd had none, not a one, about Chloe's paternity.

Lucie turned from watching the Realtor's car vanish down the street to study father and daughter. There really was no denying the truth.

Edna hadn't said a word to Ryder. Had she alerted

the rest of the town? It didn't look like it. Mrs. Carlini hadn't known. And the two women were supposedly close friends.

As Lucie stared, Chloe turned to Ryder. "You're a good weeder, mister," she said, her voice solemn, her eyes owlish again. "You're a good helper, too. Wanna be my daddy?"

Ryder's gray-blue and Lucie's amber-green eyes crashed.

Now what was she going to do?

Chapter Eight

Lucie glanced at Ryder only to find him looking at her, a hint of panic in his expression. She didn't quite panic but she didn't know how to proceed any more than he did. She shrugged and shook her head.

Chloe's sweet voice pierced the silence. "I'll be real good—I promise. I'll even eat yucky green things— won't like 'em, but I'll eat 'em. Please? Will you be my daddy?"

Tears stung Lucie's eyes and a lump lodged in her throat. She fell back and landed on the weeds again. "Oh, honey," she croaked.

"Chloe," Ryder said, his voice just as rough. He sat on the freshly cleared patch of dirt.

Their daughter stood between them, staring from silent adult to silent adult, questions in her eyes.

Lucie reached out, but Ryder was closer. He extended his large hand and Chloe placed her much smaller one in it. With impressive gentleness, he drew her in front of him, captured a loose curl with a finger and then smoothed it behind her ear.

He turned to Lucie, the clear question in his gaze. As a tear rolled down her cheek, she nodded and smiled.

He had the right to answer as he wished. She owed him that much.

"I have a story for you," he told Chloe. "It's a story about a mommy and a daddy who were lost, but only from each other. They had a little girl who lived with the mommy, but the little girl very much wanted a daddy. One day, after trying very hard, the mommy found the daddy. She took the little girl on a long, long trip to where the daddy lived—"

"Me!" Chloe said. "That's me. I don't have a daddy and Mama took me on a long, long trip and you live here…did we find you? Are you my daddy?"

Ryder swallowed hard. "Yes, Chloe. You found me. I'm your daddy."

Chloe's eyes, identical to those hidden behind the sunglasses, opened wide. "Oh!"

Suddenly shy, she stared at Ryder, fascinated, clearly trying to grasp the situation. Lucie didn't blame her for her hesitation. Lucie was an adult, one of the two responsible for their awkward circumstances, and she still struggled to comprehend it all. But one thing was clear.

"It's okay," she said. "Ryder is your daddy, honey. You don't have to keep looking anymore."

A look of delight brightened the little girl's face. "See? Jesus *did* answer my prayers. He brought me my daddy."

"Something like that," Ryder said, a smile tipping his lips. "Now don't you think we should go celebrate? Like at the diner?" He turned to Lucie. "Somewhere other than a messy corner on Main Street?"

She narrowed her gaze. "It's not quite time, and I have plenty of weeds to pull." She yanked another prime example to punctuate her words.

And to cover the overwhelming emotion the moment had evoked in her. She wasn't ready to let him see how much it meant that he accepted their daughter. And that Chloe responded in kind.

He stood, still holding Chloe's hand. "I don't think—"

"Well, hello there!" Sam Porter, the owner of Pen and Paper, said. "I see you've met our mayor."

Before Lucie could find the composure to speak, he continued, "And it looks as though…" Confusion crinkled his forehead. "He's put you both to work already?"

With what seemed to Lucie like excessive haste, Ryder clapped the dirt and bits of greenery from his hands. "I certainly did not put them to work. On the contrary. I hiked over the fence to try and talk Lucie out of tackling this mess."

She stood as well. "How can I not do something for this wonderful place? It's an absolute disgrace. When I finally get my hands on its miserable, neglectful owner, I'm going to…I'll…well, I'm not sure what I'll do. But believe me, it won't be pretty."

Sam looked from Lucie to Ryder, even more confusion on his craggy face. "Gotta say, I'd love a front seat for that." Before Ryder or Lucie could speak, he tapped the brim of his baseball cap. "I'll leave you to your work now. Hope I see you again soon."

"Wait!" Chloe said. "We are friends, right?"

Sam smiled broadly. "Of course we are, Chloe."

She went right up to him, the fence between them, then crooked an index finger to beckon him close. As he leaned toward her, she stood on tiptoe. "I got a secret that's not a secret anymore. Jesus found the daddy my mama lost." She pointed at Ryder. "See?"

Lucie nearly groaned. The expression on poor Sam's face gave her a foretaste of what was to come once the rest of Lyndon Point learned the truth.

"Your daddy?" the older man said, his gaze now on Ryder.

Who ran a finger along his collar as if it had just become tight. "It's a long story, Sam. But she's right. She's mine."

"You know I have a good ear and plenty of time, son. You can make use of either whenever you want." Sam turned to Lucie. "You, too. Most folks say I'm a good friend. I'm here if you need me."

Lucie's cheeks burned, but beyond her embarrassment, it was gratitude for the man's acceptance and his generous offer that truly warmed her. "I'll remember that."

As Sam sauntered away, awkwardness descended. "Maybe you're right," she told Ryder. "We should head to lunch now."

She picked up her purse and slipped it onto her shoulder, reached for Chloe's hand and, with the little fingers wrapped in hers, turned to leave. But right away she realized they still had the rusty gate to maneuver.

A sideways glance showed Ryder watching Sam's departure. When he turned back to her and Chloe, he let out a short, quiet exhale. He took off his sunglasses, rubbed the back of his neck, shook his head and grimaced.

Lucie reached out to him, paused. As much as she longed for even that simple contact, as much as he still drew her, she knew Ryder was dangerous for her peace of mind. She withdrew her hand and said, "I have to ask. Are you…will your…constituents hold—" she gestured toward Chloe "—all this against you? Will it change their opinion of you?"

His blue-gray eyes met hers. "I don't know. And I'm not sure I care a whole lot what anyone might think. I mean, I do care because I represent this town and I want to succeed at my job, but in the end, some things are more important than others." His gaze fell on Chloe, who was again focused on her leaf-stripping efforts, and seemed oblivious to the charged atmosphere around them.

Something melted in the vicinity of Lucie's heart at the expression on Ryder's face. He stood there, tall and athletic, with a natural power that seemed to flow toward her. At the same time, the wonder on his features brought gentleness to his strong features, a glow to his blue-gray gaze.

At that moment, a longing so fierce swelled within her that Lucie had to use all her strength to keep from reaching out to Ryder, from slipping her hand in his to watch their daughter in wonder. She'd often seen proud parents sharing such moments, and she'd wished for Ryder's presence in their lives.

She was thrilled he responded to Chloe with such deep feelings.

She recognized what he felt at that moment. She'd spent the last six years studying their daughter with the same amazement she read on his face. A child was a blessing, an exceptional creation. And Ryder was only now discovering Chloe and the gift she represented. At least they could share that much. If not much else. Not after this time.

She wasn't, however, sure she wanted the whole town to march by and discover the truth just yet. She also wondered if either Edna or Sam would spread the word.

"It's—" Lucie's voice cracked with emotion. She cleared her throat and tried again. "I think we should head over to the diner. There's always the possibility of a meltdown if meals are delayed. Trust me. You don't want to see a Chloe meltdown. Not after I made you watch mine."

He grinned. "A Chloe meltdown might not be the best of beginnings."

Lucie tugged her purse strap higher up on her shoulder. "Come on, Chloe." She held out a hand. "Let's go get lunch."

Chloe tipped her head back to peer out from under the purple visor. "But we're not done yet, Mama. You always say I gotta finish what I start."

There were times when Lucie's diligence came back to bite her. Like it just had.

At her side, Ryder muffled a chuckle. She spun to face him. "Oh, no. Don't you laugh."

He laughed harder.

She crossed her arms and gave him a knowing look. "Okay, Ryder. You think it's funny, huh? Just wait until you're at the receiving end of a Chloe-ism. Trust me. You won't be laughing then."

"You've got to admit," he said, his pride unmistakable, "she's pretty clever."

Lucie's turn to chuckle. "You're telling me? I won't debate your point. But just you wait, Ryder. Just you wait." She turned to Chloe. "Don't worry, honey. I know we're not done here. We'll come back later. But now it's time for lunch."

Chloe stood and, with a gesture that mirrored Ryder's earlier one, clapped the dirt and debris from her hands. "Can I have—"

"Chicken nuggets and *barbecue* sauce," Ryder said, his eyes twinkling with mischief.

"Mmm-hmm!" She held out her hand to Ryder. "I love barber cube sauce, Mr. Daddy."

Lucie watched surprise dart across Ryder's face. But only for a moment. With a glance toward her, and only after her encouraging nod, he took the still grimy fingers in his.

"I'll tell you a secret," he said to Chloe. "I kinda like barbecue sauce, too."

At the gate, he picked up his daughter like any father would. Chloe wrapped her arm around his neck and continued to chatter about macaroni and cheese, "smashed taters" and the rest of her favorite foods as if Ryder had been carrying her from birth. A knot tightened in Lucie's throat as she watched father and daughter do something so normal, so right, but something they'd never had the chance to do before.

She wished…no! Wishes were worthless at this point. Two months ago she had set a plan in motion. She'd prayed, turned to the Lord for guidance and now she had to step into the future. A future where Ryder would play an enormous part.

But not at Lucie's side.

The stray thought stunned her. A random part of her still wished a future for herself and Ryder was possible. But she didn't think it was. Ryder hadn't shown any sign of similar thoughts.

It surprised her how much that hurt.

Before her eyes could flood with the tears scalding her lids, she followed Ryder and Chloe. She hiked up one leg at the gate, but wobbled on her other leg and fought to keep her balance. Before she could swing over the rusty metal, Ryder set Chloe down and steadied Lucie with a firm hand at the small of her back.

The warmth of his touch, the awareness of his strength, ran through Lucie. She shivered.

"Are you cold?" he asked.

She blushed. "N-no! I…ah…shuddered at the thought of the rusty stains that fence could leave on my pants."

As soon as she spoke, she wanted to take the words back. She saw the disbelief on Ryder's face as he studied her chocolate-colored pants. Her cheeks burned hotter still.

She scrambled over the fence to the sidewalk, where

she busied herself with cleaning a smear of dirt off Chloe's cheek. Anything not to have to look at Ryder.

They walked to the corner, where the traffic light turned against them. Lucie cast a final glance at the raggedy house, drew a deep breath and turned to Ryder again. "It's way past time you told me the name of the owner."

A moment crawled by.

And another.

Still one more heartbeat oozed past before Ryder pushed his sunglasses more firmly up the bridge of his nose. Even though the glasses blocked her view of his eyes, Lucie couldn't miss the tightening of his jaw and the thinning of his lips.

They waited for the slowest light in history to change. Without exchanging a word.

When Lucie had enough, she prodded. "I don't see why you and your aunt have to make such a huge mystery about this." She pushed a loose lock of hair behind her ear. "I'm sure I can ask anyone in town—other than you and Edna—and they'll tell me who owns the house."

"The town."

"Yes. Anyone I ask in town will tell me."

She hoped.

The light changed, and Ryder took Chloe's left hand while Lucie took the right. Unexpected emotion diverted her thoughts from the house to the magnitude of the moment. If someone didn't know better, they would see the three of them as the perfect family. The perfect family they might have been....

The knot formed in her throat again.

"That wasn't what I meant," Ryder said, his terse voice cutting into her poignant thoughts. "I meant that the town owns the house."

She tripped on the curb.

Stumbled up onto the sidewalk.

Turned on him. "How can that be? This town is gorgeous. I can't believe a community that takes so much pride in its downtown would ever let a house get to that condition."

A muscle twitched in his lean cheek. "It's not that simple, Lucie. There are conditions attached to the ownership of the property."

"Conditions? What kind of conditions call for a place to rot?"

"That's not what I mean, and you know it."

"That's what it sounds like."

He shook his head. "You only heard what fits your version of the situation. Here's the deal. The house was left to the town as part of a late resident's will. The will has a specific clause about the use of the property. For anything to be done to the house or the grounds, two particular parties must be in complete agreement."

"So what's the problem? Why don't you bring them out here to have a look at the place? Any reasonable person would realize maintaining the property in good condition makes sense. It's only logical, practical."

His Adam's apple bobbed as he swallowed hard.

Before he could answer, Chloe piped up. "Mama! Can I have a gumball? That machine over there has lots and lots."

"No—"

"Sure—"

Lucie glared at Ryder, but frustration spiked again when she couldn't read his expression behind the dark sunglasses. How dare he? Chloe was her daughter.

Then, to her even greater frustration, she realized he had every right to offer his input. Chloe was his daughter, too.

Gritting her teeth, she eked out a response. "How about a compromise?"

A glance out the corner of her eyes revealed Ryder's eyebrows arched over his glasses. Good. She'd surprised him, caught him off guard.

She went on. "How about if you get a gumball now, but you save it for after your lunch?"

Ryder grinned.

Chloe didn't. "How come you always make me do something boring before I can do something fun?"

Lucie fought a smile. "Because, my darling daughter, that's what life's about. If you do what you *have* to do first, later on you can relax and have fun while you do what you *want* to do. That way you won't have to worry about what you didn't do."

Chloe crossed her arms and tipped her head back. From under the bill of her visor, her eyes pinned Lucie as they so often did. "Are you gonna make me eat green stuff again?"

This time, Ryder laughed out loud.

Lucie didn't. "What do you think, Chloe? What's the right thing to do?"

"Ma-*maaaaa!*" She glared at Lucie, then slanted a look at the gumball machine. "That's not fair!"

"Sure it is, honey. You know what's right."

After long moments of deliberation, Chloe turned to Ryder. He gave a helpless shrug and shook his head. She sighed and faced Lucie again. "Oh, okay. But I *hate* green stuff." She held out a hand, took the coin from Lucie and stomped off to the gumball machine.

She paused, turned to Ryder. "You don't like yucky green stuff, either, right, Mr. Daddy?"

At Lucie's side, Ryder chuckled softly. "She really is mine, isn't she?"

Lucie studied him from beneath an arched brow. "What gives it away? The green stuff on the plate or her stubbornness?"

"Ouch!" He held out both hands in self-defense. "Oh, the green stuff. Absolutely. No doubt about it."

"There's an old cliché that fits your answer, you know. You're protesting too much."

Ryder walked to Chloe's side. "You know, Chloe, green stuff's good for you. Your mama's right."

Chloe snorted and marched up the steps on her own.

He hurried to the diner door and held it open, the mischievous grin Lucie had fallen for on display. "I just realized how hungry I am. And we don't want Chloe to have a meltdown, now, do we?"

Lucie stood her ground. "About that other topic—the house?"

His grin vanished.

"You haven't told me the name of the other party named in the will. The one who must agree with the town so that something can happen."

He stopped, froze in the doorway.

Chloe tugged on his pants leg. "I'm sooooo hungry for chicken nuggets, Mr. Daddy. Are you?"

As she scooted around to stand at his side, Lucie kept her gaze on his face, glaring at the obstructive sunglasses. "Ryder?" she said. "Who is the other party named in that will?"

Once again, the muscle in Ryder's lean jaw twitched and his lips thinned into a tight line of displeasure.

Lucie stared. Father and daughter, the two of them so alike, stared back at her. As seconds ticked by, the image of the smiling Chloe at her father's side, both of them framed by the diner's doorway, penetrated Lucie's frustration. She realized that moment would stay with her forever.

"Who, Ryder?" Lucie pushed, more determined by the minute. "Who do I need to speak to about the house?"

That seemed to jolt him out of his frozen state. He turned, held his hand out to Chloe and stepped into the diner.

Lucie caught up to them and slipped inside. As she parted her lips to speak, Ryder glanced over his shoulder, the buglike sunglasses now gone. Icy intensity burned in his blue-gray eyes.

"Me."

Lucie stumbled. Again. "You?"

He walked on as though she hadn't spoken. But his single word hit her like a punch in the gut and echoed in her head. Hurt and anger reared up to do battle.

Ryder? *He* was the one keeping that lovely, lovely old home in that terrible condition?

Hot words rushed to be voiced, but a glance at her daughter's smiling face held them back. Oh, yes. Lucie was angry. She was furious. But she was also a mother. Another argument between her parents, this one more personal, with the potential to escalate to greater heights, was not in Chloe's best interests.

Chloe liked Ryder, and Lucie wanted them to build a good relationship. Was she willing to sacrifice her perfect location for that budding relationship?

She followed father and daughter to a booth in the back of the diner. She sighed.

Yes, she was.

Her foolishness had cheated them out of too many years. In spite of Ryder's refusal to discuss the Victorian, Lucie was in Lyndon Point to stay. They'd have plenty of time to hash out the details of the house, its condition and her determination to turn it into her new store.

Later. When Chloe wasn't around.

"Yes, Ryder," Lucie said, her words crisp, clear and clipped. "Let's eat. For now."

He was in trouble. Ryder knew it.

The situation with the Victorian put him in a terrible position. He had to keep the house available for the day his sister came to her senses and tired of "following her bliss," as she'd put it. One day, the instability would get to Dee and she'd come back to Lyndon Point. The house, Dee's dream home, had to be ready for her to move in and restore.

Even if that meant argument after argument with Lucie. Sooner or later, he'd explain himself to her. She'd understand when he did.

He hoped. The last thing he wanted was to reveal to Lucie how badly he bombed in yet another relationship.

But the house wasn't his only problem. Not only had he started their lunch off on the proverbial wrong foot, but he'd also bombed in a couple of minor skirmishes with Chloe.

"Jell-O's green, Mama," she argued. "That's my green food for lunch."

Ryder muffled his laugh with his napkin.

That bit of five-year-old logic stumped Lucie. He sure hadn't known how to counter it.

Somehow, Chloe knew where to turn. "It's green, Mr. Daddy, right?"

Still no fan of broccoli, and faced by the double female scrutiny, Ryder experienced a sudden need to use the restroom. By the time he returned, a cup of lime gelatin cubes jiggled in front of Chloe, next to her small plate of chicken nuggets and barber cube sauce.

The meal continued to be strained. In an effort to get

past the tension between him and Lucie, he focused on getting to know Chloe better. And he realized how awkward he felt around his child.

Not only had he committed the faux pas of running and leaving Lucie to cope with Chloe's green aversion on her own, but he also blundered when it came to conversational topics—he had no idea what interested five-year-old girls.

Chloe carried the exchange.

Ryder couldn't hold up his end. He knew nothing about *Phineas and Ferb*—apparently a popular television program among five-year-olds. He knew even less about princesses and their preferences.

What bugged him most was Lucie's enjoyment of his discomfort. He didn't blame her, but he didn't like how it made him feel, either.

When they stood to leave the diner, his aunt Edna walked in. She waved to Ryder, greeted Lucie and dropped down to Chloe's level. "Hi, sweetie," she said. "Did you have a good lunch?"

Chloe looked to Lucie for approval. Lucie nodded and Chloe marched over to Aunt Edna, her gumball-stained hand outstretched. "I did. I had chicken nuggets and barber cube sauce and found my daddy that Mama lost and, see?" She tipped her head toward Ryder. "He likes nuggets and barber cube sauce, too." To Lucie she said, "*Now* I can have my gumball, right?"

Ryder glanced at Aunt Edna to see her reaction.

She smiled, but her gray eyes spoke volumes about the grilling he was in for. At a later point.

He sighed. And nodded.

Aunt Edna then dutifully admired the somewhat melted,

red-glazed ball. Ryder watched, envying his aunt's ease with Chloe.

"Is it a female thing?" he asked Lucie.

"Is what a female thing? Talking?"

He shrugged. "Sure, talking is supposed to come easier to women, but I meant how much easier it is for Aunt Edna to talk to Chloe than it is for me."

"I don't think it's a female thing. Does Edna have children?"

"My cousin, Amanda."

"There you go. She has experience communicating with a little girl. That's all it is."

"Okay. I'll buy that." Chloe grinned at something his aunt said, the expression brightening her face and reaching deep into Ryder's heart. "It's going to take me some time to catch up. But I will get beyond my awkwardness around Chloe. I do want to be her daddy."

Standing tall, Lucie gave him a tight smile. "Think how much time you'll have to spend with Chloe once we settle down nearby. It really would be in your best interest to help me persuade the town to sell me the house."

He should have seen that one coming. While he knew Lucie had a point—about her and Chloe settling in town—he couldn't let her think she was about to buy the house. She had to put it out of her mind.

"Sorry. It's not for sale."

"But—"

"It's not even open for discussion."

He saw the flash of anger in her eyes. He winced. If he hadn't had an important reason to keep the house available, he would have wavered. He would much rather see Lucie smile than bite down on her bottom lip and rake him with a furious stare.

"Even if it helps Chloe and me to settle down in town?

Even if it makes it easier for you to spend time with Chloe?"

When he didn't respond, she gave a sharp nod. "How serious are you about building a close relationship with Chloe?"

Chapter Nine

Ryder's world tilted on its axis. He looked at Chloe, and a wave of emotion rocked him. He wanted to spend time with his daughter, to build a strong, close relationship with her. But at the same time, he could never forget the last time he'd seen Dee or the anger at their parting. There was also the last time he'd seen his parents and his late grandparents. Even more to the point, he remembered the many times he'd promised to take care of his younger sister.

And his colossal failure to do so.

Regret left a bitter taste.

"No," he said, his voice low but determined. "It's not going to happen. Please find another place for your store. Check out the Johnsons' cottage. They need to sell."

She compressed her lips for a moment. "Edna already showed it to me," she said, her voice tight and cool. "The cottage is too small for Chloe and me. It won't work."

Ryder narrowed his eyes. "You're smart, and you say you want to become a businesswoman." He shrugged a shoulder. "Make it work."

Enough. He was done. He didn't want to argue anymore. Not about this, not while his emotions were roiling inside him. Even though he knew it wasn't fair to Lucie, he turned on his heel and walked away before she had a chance to respond.

Then he paused, glanced over his shoulder at the stunned expression on his daughter's face. Dismay hit hard.

"Goodbye, Chloe. I hope you find more special rocks soon."

Feeling like a fool, he headed toward his office.

On his way there, he wondered if Lucie would hold his refusal to sell against him. Would she let it interfere with his plans to spend time with Chloe?

What would he do if she did?

Lucie pried open first one and then the other eyelid. Morning had come too soon. "Ugh."

Now she knew that, contrary to the cliché, not everything improved with age. Ryder's easygoing nature seemed to have taken a turn for the worse since Baja. These days he struck her as an inflexible naysayer.

From within her cozy cocoon of silky sheets and light blanket, Lucie watched the sunrise outside her hotel window, a strange event, memorable because of the vast amount of gray. If the hotel alarm clock hadn't been beaming the time of day from the nearby bedside table, she would have had a hard time telling whether it was morning, noon or evening. The Seattle area's notorious weather had made its appearance.

Where had yesterday's brilliant blue sky gone?

Probably to the same place where Ryder's stubbornness had sent her sunny, optimistic mood.

The Victorian was perfect for her needs. She knew it. Even though Ryder and the city council had allowed it to become a mess, Lucie was ready to invest her nest egg to restore the house and turn it into the beautiful quilt and needle arts store it could one day be. But for some baffling reason, Ryder had made his intentions clear. He was going to block her efforts.

Why?

Lucie sighed. Ryder also had no intention of telling her why.

She glanced at the door to the suite's living room, from where the sound of children's programming reached her. It appeared that Chloe had turned down the volume. Time to get up and see what kind of trouble her daughter might have found.

As she sat up, Lucie groaned. Every part of her body objected, and her head felt fuzzy, as though she were coming down with a cold. She couldn't blame a virus for the cotton-brain sensation or her widespread stiffness. She hadn't slept much. Instead, she'd spent the night flopping from side to side, looking for a comfortable position, with no success. But neither the bed nor her position had really lacked comfort. Her situation chafed more than the infamous pea had irritated the fairy-tale princess.

What would make Ryder refuse to even consider her offer to buy? Why was he so inflexible on that point?

Would he be as obstinate when they disagreed over something that affected Chloe?

As Lucie glanced out the window again, she saw her well-used Bible where she'd set it on the nightstand by the alarm clock. She reached for it, opened to the Psalms, but before she started reading, turned to the Father in prayer.

"Help me here, Lord. Please give me the right words, the right way to help Ryder see my side of things. I'm sure You've brought me here, but for me to be able to stay, You know I need somewhere to live and a way to earn a living. Help me figure out what I should do...."

Minutes later, as she read through the twenty-third Psalm, one of Lucie's favorite passages of scripture and one of the most encouraging ones, too, Edna's laughing expression came to mind. The Realtor seemed to have no problem with their situation. On the contrary. Edna seemed to like the idea of her nephew as a father.

Edna could become a powerful ally in her battle for the Victorian. Since Lucie had agreed to meet her that day at the real estate office to search the multiple listing again, she saw no reason why she couldn't ask Edna for information. She hoped this time Edna would prove more willing to reveal what lay behind Ryder's refusals.

She had no problem appealing to Edna's love for her nephew, to her appreciation of Chloe's antics and even to the pleasure the Realtor had displayed the day before when Chloe had confirmed her suspicions.

She thought Ryder's aunt might be more likely now to share at least some of what she knew than she had been before.

Lucie didn't want to dig too deeply into Edna's motives. Mrs. Carlini's matchmaking efforts at the restaurant remained a too-vivid memory. Ryder had described Edna and the pizza parlor maven as cronies. Lucie wouldn't enjoy more of the same, but she was willing to put up with the embarrassment if it meant she'd get somewhere with her future plans.

Even knowing Ryder had no place in that future.

Her future.

"I'm going to find you the perfect place," Edna said. "It's just going to take me longer than you or I would like."

A strange calm enveloped Lucie. Here was the opening for which she'd waited since her devotions that morning. "The lack of other practical properties only makes me more determined. I've already found the perfect place, Edna."

The Realtor averted her gaze, but didn't respond.

"I don't want to insult your intelligence," Lucie added, "so I'm going to lay it all out on the table."

That brought Edna's gaze—reluctantly—back to Lucie's face. "I'd never think you were trying to insult me."

"Then let's get beyond the awkwardness, okay?"

Edna glanced at Chloe, who was playing with a generous assortment of toys in the corner of the office.

"Yes," Lucie said in a quiet voice. "She is his."

"She looks just like him, especially when he was that age. But…?"

"It's a boring story of two college kids on spring break too stupid to know any better." She pushed a lock of hair behind her ear, gathered her thoughts again. "We never exchanged the necessary information, and when I knew I was expecting, I had no way to find him."

Edna looked startled, but before she could probe, Lucie continued. "I want you to know, I did try, but I had very little to go on. Until I saw his picture on Lyndon Point's website, I was afraid I'd never have the chance to introduce them."

"All those years…how sad. For both of them."

"It was too long. But we're working on a better future, and I promise we'll get there. Sooner rather than later." Lucie breathed deep again. It was time to get down to business. "You can see now why it's so important for me to open my store here in town. It's only fair for the two of them to live close enough so they can spend lots of time together."

Edna studied her from under an arched brow. "And you?"

Lucie chose to misunderstand. "And I have a business to open. I can't support Chloe and me if I can't earn a living.

I think you know as well as I do that the Victorian is the perfect place for us."

The older woman seemed about to call Lucie on her blatant sidestep, but then only gave a long exhale. "It very well could be."

When Lucie went to press her advantage, Edna lifted a hand to stop her. "But it's not up to me to do anything about it. I have no say in the house's fate."

"I'll take your word for it, even though Ryder's love for you is clear, and you probably have more sway with him than you know." She chose her next words with care. "Maybe you can still help me. Could you please answer some questions for me?"

With an impressive show of dignity, Edna sat taller and squared her shoulders. "I won't betray my nephew, Lucie, so please don't ask me to do that again."

"Fair enough," she conceded. "What about the will? What can you tell me about the clause Ryder mentioned? It sounds crazy to me. He said the house belongs to Lyndon Point, but he still calls the shots? Doesn't town government, a city council or something, handle that kind of thing?"

"Kermit Hooper, the former owner, was one of a kind." A fond smile played on Edna's lips. "He was unique, but way ahead of his time. He invested in Bill Gates's dreams back in the early days, and you can imagine what Microsoft's success did for his investment. By the time the Victorian came up for sale, Kermit decided to indulge himself with the one thing he'd always wanted. He bought the house from the ladies who'd tried to run a travel agency out of the place."

"A travel agency?"

"As you can imagine, in our age of the information superhighway, there wasn't much need for a travel agency in Lyndon Point. Because of the women's depleted funds, the house had fallen into disrepair by the time they called it quits. Kermit paid a fair price, but he still got the place for a song."

"Didn't this Kermit care enough to maintain the place once he bought it?"

"Kermit was a cantankerous coot, no doubt about it, but he wasn't a bad sort. Even though he loved the house, he found out he had cancer three months after he signed the papers. He fought like the ornery mule he'd always been, but in the end, the disease had progressed too far by the time of the diagnosis. He died almost three years ago and left the place to the town. The complexities of probating his will took forever and it's only recently been settled."

"I'm sure he never thought Lyndon Point would let it rot."

"You're right. He thought it would make a wonderful museum to feature Puget Sound history. He never much liked the idea of housing the historical society in the other half of the post-office building where it has been for years."

Lucie had followed the story so far. At that point, however, her questions began to multiply. "Is there something wrong with the historical-society location?"

Edna shook her head. "It just isn't what he thought a proper museum should be."

"And after the town inherited the house, was it strapped for the cash to convert the house into a museum?"

The Realtor looked uncomfortable. "I'm not sure. I'm not saying the town's rolling in dough, but I do believe its finances are on solid-enough footing. After all, Ryder's kept the books since he came home from college and he's very good at what he does. Anyway, no one's in a hurry to move the historical society to the house."

Unless Lucie was much mistaken, Edna was holding

back more than what she'd revealed. Lucie told herself to be patient. She had, after all, just arrived in town, while Edna was Ryder's aunt.

She shifted in her wingback chair, crossed her left leg over her right and tried again. "Are you telling me the town doesn't care that the house looks like that? Or is Ryder really the one who insists on neglecting it so much that it's going to cave into the foundation before much longer?"

Edna darted a look out the office window. She picked up a stack of papers, tapped them against the desk to straighten the edges. She opened a drawer, withdrew a fat manila folder.

As Lucie's irritation threatened to erupt, Edna rose and headed toward a small table at the left of the door where a coffeemaker had finished brewing moments earlier. She poured a mug of coffee, then held the carafe out to Lucie. "Want some?"

Patience, Lucie. Patience.

"No, thank you, Edna. But I would like some of those answers. Doesn't City Council have any interest in the house? If, in the end, it's Ryder who insists on destroying a town landmark."

A blatantly dismissive wave added to Lucie's frustration. Instead of answering, the Realtor sipped coffee. Sipped some more. When she finally put the mug down on the desk, she smiled at Lucie, the strain obvious in the tight corners of her lips.

Lucie waited. And waited.

Edna tapped the fat folder. "I'm sure they do. I have here a handful of new properties about to go on the market, ones we haven't entered into the multiple-listing service yet. Since I didn't negotiate the representation for them, I haven't seen the details. I'd like us to check and see if there's something we should tour—"

Lucie sighed. "Oh, Edna, I thought we'd moved past this kind of thing."

The Realtor's eyes widened in distress. She nodded, but didn't speak.

"Okay, okay." Lucie took the papers. "I'll give these a chance."

Before Edna went off on that topic, Lucie continued. "Why don't you tell me how the town government works? I know Ryder's the mayor, but I can't see him as a dictatorial ruler, holding the rest of the town hostage to his decrees."

Indignation gave Edna back her characteristic zest. "Why, of course he's not! He's a wonderful mayor, and he always takes the time to listen to all sides of the issues. He's well liked, and more important, well respected. You should see how he handles himself and the town's business during Council meetings."

Lucie's breath snagged in her throat. Her thoughts sped up. A plan began to gel. "I would think Council meetings are…interesting."

Edna's relief rushed out in a laugh. "That's one way of putting it. Hilarious or even insane are others."

Somehow hilarity, insanity and Ryder didn't sound like they could go together. Lucie arched a brow. "How so?"

"Some of the items on the agenda are at best unusual."

"And at worst downright weird, right?"

"Even off the wall." Her eyes twinkled at the memories. "Oh, the stories I could tell."

"But it's probably best if I see for myself, right? Especially since I want to join the town's business community."

"That's the right idea," Edna said. "And you won't have to wait long. The next meeting is tomorrow night at seven in Council Chambers. A fancy name for a biggish room at our *small* City Hall." Her amusement grew. "I hope they behave and don't horrify you too much."

"Trust me, Edna. It's going to take a whole lot more than contentious local-government wrangling to scare me away. I didn't move cross-country to be put off by zoning squabbles or bogus grievances."

"There have been many times we've all wished it all boiled down to zoning squabbles, believe me." Edna's emphatic nod made her spiky silver hair quiver. "But you'll see."

Lucie stood, certain she wouldn't get any more information from Edna. At least, not that day. But tomorrow... the town's council meeting held a great deal of promise.

As she led Chloe out of the real estate office, her plan took shape. Lucie smiled. There were many ways to approach a problem. It looked as though she had come up with a new one.

She'd be ready for that city council meeting the next day.

"Order!" Ryder called. "Order!"

The roar of complaints regrouped into a buzz of discontent. In spite of the differences between them, Lucie couldn't help the swell of sympathy for Ryder. And admiration. He maintained his composure in spite of the madness in the large room.

"Mr. Haaraldson," Ryder said in a patient voice, "you have the floor."

A grizzled senior in ancient overalls and green plaid shirt bolted from his chair and approached the council table. "Like I told ya already, Ryder—er, Mr. Mayor. Dogs downtown are nothing but a health hazard. Them mutts go around—er—messing. It's what dogs do, you know? Then the rest of us gotta clean up before we step in it. Ban 'em, I say. No more dogs downtown."

"You can't do that!" This dissenter's wavy hair and batik dress quivered with her outrage. "What about service dogs? You can't ban them."

That stumped the man. For a second. "I still don't want to have to dodge piles of *fertilizer* all over town. Smells, too."

Other concerned citizens argued in favor of pet owners who always carried and used disposal bags when they walked their pets, while a handful made their case on behalf of pet-phobes.

A tiny woman in a fluttery floral frock suitable for afternoon tea spoke up next. "Animal Control really should do more than drive through town in their new truck, Mr. Mayor. They ought to put leash and scoop ordinance violators in jail."

Upon her pronouncement, deafening silence descended on the room. Little by little, whispers rose from the gathered citizens and grew to a roar again.

Ryder plied his gavel.

The lady added, "I propose a canine jail sentence at the kennel where you house strays. The owners would realize the town means business. In addition, the town would charge owners for the food the dogs eat while confined."

A roar of approval arose.

Followed by shouts of dissent.

Lucie glanced at Ryder. A muscle twitched in his cheek, and she suspected he was close to his breaking point. As though he'd heard her thought, he smacked down his gavel.

"Now that we've heard all sides of the dog issue," he said, "the city needs to study the legal implications of tonight's request. We'll put the dogs back on the agenda once we have the town attorney's advice. Do I have a motion to table the discussion until the study is done?"

A woman from the far side of the room so moved.

A raspy male voice seconded the motion.

A debate on trees followed dogs. That measure was also tabled for further study. Then budgetary concerns followed the tree dilemma—to Lucie's relief. The trees and dogs had made her head spin. On the other hand, she figured she could deal with the town's budget.

The meeting dragged on. She hoped Chloe and her babysitter were having a better time.

Before too long, she'd learned the minutiae of job descriptions, their accompanying salaries, the latest increase—to the penny—of Lyndon Point's electrical bills and the exorbitant cost of scraping barnacles from the underside of the Lyndon Point pier. Unfortunately, some residents considered that a ridiculous, unnecessary expense. Others felt the sight of the barnacles at low tide negatively affected the beauty of the town.

The haranguing put at least two men to sleep.

Lucie fought to avoid joining the snoozers.

Finally, after what felt like an eternity, Ryder cracked the gavel again. "Any new business from the assembly?"

Lucie blinked and shook herself. Time had come for the reason why she had subjected herself to the last two hours and forty-seven painful minutes. She stood, laptop open to her PowerPoint presentation, a thick stack of printed flyers in her other hand.

"Yes, Mr. Mayor," she said. "I'd like a moment to address everyone who has attended this meeting because they care about their town."

Ryder gaped.

Lucie could see he wanted to cut her off, but his natural

politeness, his position as mayor and the by-now intrigued crowd kept him from giving in to his urge.

His chest expanded with a deep breath. He narrowed his eyes, laced his fingers. Lucie had to wonder if his gestures were to keep from banging that gavel until she either sat again or walked out.

"You may have the floor, Ms. Adams," he finally said in that too serious, tense voice of his.

As she walked to the front of the chamber, Lucie prayed. She asked the Lord to calm her nerves, to help her choose her words, to open the hearts of those at the meeting and especially to help Ryder see her side.

She faced the crowd. "First of all, I would like to introduce myself. I'm Lucie Adams, and I've moved to your lovely town to make it my home." She set the laptop on the table right in front of Ryder, divided her fliers into stacks and then handed them to a handful of attendees. "Please pass those around for me. I'd like to join your business community, and the fliers show what I propose."

Chapter Ten

Ryder's jaw hurt from biting down hard for so long. He'd known Lucie was smart. He just hadn't thought she'd be so sly as well. To think she'd invaded his territory with her determination to buy Great-great-grandfather Percy's house.

He'd told her to put the idea out of her mind—and not just once. In spite of that, she'd had the nerve to show up at this insane meeting. He'd had a rough time concentrating on the agenda, and not because of the dog issues or the tree fight. His distraction had been Lucie's fault.

From the moment she walked in, it was as though he'd developed some kind of radar. He'd known where she sat, and his eyes had seemed to take on a life of their own. They'd zoomed in on her time and time again, even when he should have focused on reining in the rampant lunacy the different factions ricocheted through Council Chambers.

He had to give Lucie credit. She'd made an excellent presentation, clear, cohesive and appealing. The intelligence he'd known she possessed had shined when she'd revealed diagrams of her planned showrooms, and even more so when she'd rattled off a list of the fabric and knitting stores nearest Lyndon Point. Ryder hadn't been able to deny her claim that to satisfy her potential customers' crafty appetites, they currently had to travel to either of the two large box stores in Lynnwood. If they wanted higher-quality, more exclusive goods, they had the option of a number of single-craft shops, some again in Lynnwood, but also others in Edmonds and Everett. Her store would keep local shoppers in his town, and maybe even draw others once word of mouth got around.

She not only planned to sell the supplies, but she also wanted to offer classes in knitting, crocheting, quilting and cross-stitching. In addition, she intended to supplement the classes with weekly open gatherings, and she would reel in those would-be crafters by serving them rivers of coffee and tea supplied by Tea & Sympathy and the Point Café, and mountains of pastries from the nearby Let Them Eat Cake.

Ryder saw the women at the meeting smile, and he heard the excitement in their whispered buzz. He didn't think half of them knew one end of a knitting needle from the other, but Lucie had enticed them with the offer of training and fellowship. He suspected the latter was a greater draw than the former.

She was good.

Lucie and her shop would be a great addition to the town.

Great-great-grandfather Percy's house was perfect.

He ran a hand through his hair. His little sister had dreamed of fixing, then living in the money pit since the time she'd turned six years old. Ryder couldn't let Lucie buy it. He didn't know if Dee would show up tomorrow or the day after Lucie signed her name on the deed. He hadn't given up on finding his sister. He had to keep her house ready and waiting for her return home.

Even though it meant breaking Lucie's heart.

As she'd broken his years ago.

He looked at her. Now that he'd adjourned the meeting, a crowd of Lyndon Point's residents surrounded her. She exuded energy and knowledge.

Yes, she'd broken his heart. But in a moment of total honesty, Ryder had to admit that from what she'd said, the way she'd reacted to him since they'd bumped into each other, Lucie felt he'd broken her heart back then, too.

Talk about being torn. On the one hand, the promise of redemption and his sister's return to the family. On the other, a new relationship with Lucie and the joys of fatherhood.

In spite of everything, some part of him still held out hope for him and Lucie. He'd never forgotten their long walks on the beach in Baja. He wished there was a way forward for them.

As much as he hated to admit it, she did have a point. She needed a place for her and Chloe to live. As far as he was concerned, the closer they lived to him, the better. He didn't want to miss another moment of his daughter's life. Chloe...

And yet, there was Dee. He'd failed her once already. He had to redeem himself. That meant he had to keep Lucie from buying that house.

In the three days after the city council meeting, Lucie's irritation only grew. While she'd gone to the council chambers far too aware of Ryder's opposition to her purchase of the house, the response of the people she'd met there had buoyed her spirits. When Ryder had adjourned the meeting, a group of women had surrounded her. Each one introduced herself and gave Lucie all kinds of encouragement. Even a couple of the men, business- and property-owners all, had approached her. They'd been especially interested in cleaning up the eyesore the house had become.

When the group thinned, Lucie had started toward Ryder, cheered by the welcome she and her plans had received. But a scant five feet away, the expression on his face had frozen her in place. His anger had reached out to entangle her, and she'd been unable to confront him right then.

She'd left, headed to the hotel, and once in the room, she'd stood by Chloe's bed to watch their daughter's peaceful sleep. For the first time, she'd questioned her decision to move.

Was Ryder the man she'd hoped he would be? Would he become the loving father Chloe needed?

Still…had she made a mistake by coming to Lyndon Point?

Lucie slipped into the bathroom, washed off her makeup and changed into her pajamas before heading to bed. Once again, she struggled to find a comfortable spot. For hours, she tossed and rolled, stared at the numbers as they changed on the alarm clock's LCD screen and wished she could turn on the television without disturbing Chloe. She knew by experience the sound would have lulled her to sleep before long.

At least, it always had in the past. Tonight? She had to wonder.

Frustrated, she punched the pillow. Which didn't satisfy, so she punched it again, this time harder. And got the same, ineffective result.

"Lord? Did I blow this? Should I have stayed in New York?"

She sighed. She couldn't have stayed. Chloe needed her father. And Ryder needed to know Chloe. But now Lucie needed a place for her shop. Would he ever change his mind about the house?

An hour later, as the thoughts continued to hound her, Lucie did a relaxation exercise she'd learned during pregnancy. Beginning with her toes, she relaxed every muscle, one by one....

The next morning, she remembered only reaching her knees. And her conviction was reinforced.

"Nope," she murmured as she gathered fresh clothes. "I'm not the one who's made the mistake. Everyone at that meeting last night wants my store in that house. Ryder's at least going to have to give me a better reason for his refusal than 'It's not open for discussion.'"

She would just have to find a better way to show him her side. As he spent time with Chloe, he would see how much more the two of them could share if she and Lucie lived nearby—at the house. He would understand how important it was to all three of them for Lucie to settle into the right place to live and work.

She hurried through her shower, dressed and then readied Chloe for the day. At the pool the day before, Sarah, another five-year-old girl at the hotel, had befriended Chloe. To Lucie's delight, the child's mother had invited Chloe to spend the afternoon with their family, since she and her husband were taking Sarah and their twin eight-year-old sons fishing from the town's pier. The girly-girl Chloe had surprised Lucie with her enthusiasm, and she'd agreed to the plan.

She intended to make good use of the child-free time. She was going to beard the lion in his den.

Fifteen minutes past one, Lucie walked into the offices of Lyndon Accounting at the southern end of Main Street. She didn't know what she'd expected, but the masculine elegance of the waiting room brought her up short. As did the pointed scrutiny of the woman behind the elegant walnut desk.

"May I help you?" she asked Lucie, her chocolate eyes asking more than her bland question suggested.

Lucie looked around the room, at the butter-gold-colored walls; the toffee leather sofa and camel chenille wing chairs arranged in welcoming groups; at the tone-on-tone gold-striped drapes framing the windows on either side of the front door; even at the black, gold, taupe and gray geometric rug underfoot.

Had Ryder decorated the place? If so, he had excellent taste.

"Ahem!" the woman said, raking her hand through her short hair.

Lucie blushed. "I'm here to see Ryder."

"He's busy at the moment with…a client, and he has another appointment afterward. Could I help you? Maybe pencil you in for later?"

Knowing she shouldn't, but too irritated to let her better judgment win the day, Lucie marched past the woman, having caught the strategic hesitation in her response.

Humph! The man was probably avoiding her. Everyone in Lyndon Point knew her, if for no other reason than because she was a stranger in town. They probably could pick out newcomers a mile away. He'd likely told his gatekeeper to deflect her when he saw her coming.

Squaring her shoulders, she threw open the door and stomped into the inner office.

And came to a complete halt.

Ryder wasn't alone. He had a client. As she'd been told.

Lucie blushed again, hotter this time. "Oh!"

Ryder narrowed his spectacular blue-gray eyes. "Good

afternoon." His tone of voice suggested it was anything but. No doubt due to her dramatic entrance.

"Ah...well, I needed to see you." She backed up a step. "And I guessed you'd be..." She gestured to their surroundings, as tasteful as the waiting room. "I figured you'd be here. And you are. But you're busy." Another step back. "So I'll be going now. And making an appointment."

Oh, Lord Jesus! That verse about pride and a spectacular fall? You were too, too right.

She held out a hand in a vague plea. "I'm sorry, Ryder. I should have made that appointment before I, well—" She cleared her throat, straightened her spine, stood at her full height. "That appointment I'm going to make as soon as I walk out of here. Right now—"

"Ryder?" the woman said. "Introductions, please."

He glanced at her. "Yes, Aunt Myra, this is Lucie Adams, the woman who wants to open the fabric and needle store here in Lyndon Point." He turned to Lucie. "This is my aunt Myra Sorensen, Lucie. She's my late father's youngest sister. Aunt Edna's the oldest."

Wishing she'd rushed out at least half as fast as she'd stormed in, Lucie stumbled forward, hand outstretched. The woman's firm clasp and warm smile surprised her, helped her regain her footing and impressed her. A great deal.

"Pleased to meet you," Myra Sorensen said. "Especially after all I've heard about you from Edna."

Lucie fought to stop a wince. "Nothing too awful, I hope."

"On the contrary. My sister's had nothing but compliments for you. And your little girl."

Oh, boy. Her little girl. Ryder's little girl.

No way. Not right then. Lucie wasn't going there when she was at such a disadvantage. She swallowed hard.

"Thanks, and please accept my apology for barging in like this. I don't usually impersonate a runaway train."

Myra's lively blue eyes sized her up. "Enthusiasm's not something to dismiss lightly. I think I'm going to like you."

Lucie's eyes opened wide. "On the basis of this?"

Myra laughed. "There you go. I already like you. Based on what I've heard *and* what I've seen now."

Other than finding Ryder in Lyndon Point, nothing had gone according to plan since she'd arrived. Time for retreat. "Thanks," Lucie said. "You're very kind. And I'm pleased to meet you, too. Now I'm going to leave you to continue your appointment."

"Don't give it another thought," Myra said. "We were just discussing the lousy economic climate and its effect on folks' spending. Amazing how many people with brown thumbs have suddenly become their own landscapers."

"Landscapers?" Lucie asked.

Ryder made a choked sound.

Myra waggled the file she held in her right hand. "That's what I do. And it's one of the first expenses people cut out when finances get tight."

"A landscaper," Lucie said, slowly enunciating every letter. She slanted a look at Ryder, who averted his gaze. She turned back to his aunt. "And your business has been hurt from a lack of landscaping jobs. Lawn care jobs. Groundskeeping jobs. *Weeding* jobs."

Myra looked from Lucie to Ryder, then bit her bottom lip. "Maybe I should leave—"

"No!"

"No!" Lucie's embarrassment turned to anger. "No, Myra. You were here first. But I'll be back." She shot a look at Ryder. "You can count on it."

She spun on her heel and flew out of the room, through

the waiting room and out onto the sidewalk. There, breath coming in harsh spurts, she paused, not sure what she intended to do next.

Do? She wasn't sure she could do much of anything at that moment. She was so mad at Ryder. Clearly, his aunt could have maintained the property around the Victorian. But she hadn't been hired to do the job.

Had Ryder stood in his aunt's way, too? If so, why?

Chest heaving, Lucie pondered what that meant. But no rational answer occurred to her.

As she stared at the door to Lyndon Accounting, she noticed the attractive wrought-iron bench in front of the furniture boutique next door. Okay. Sure. She knew what she was going to do. She was going to sit, gather her thoughts and wait for Myra Sorensen to come out of her nephew's office. Then Lucie would make her move.

She was going to get somewhere.

Ryder or no Ryder.

Two days later Ryder felt as though he'd heard from every last one of his excited constituents in favor of Lucie's proposed store. The onslaught had made concentrating on his clients' business tougher than it should have been.

Still, he hadn't forgotten his aunt's financial woes. He'd done his homework and had put together a funding package for Aunt Myra in spite of the distractions and her skimpy personal funds. Fortunately, her portion of the family trust's upcoming dividend payment would cover most of the landscaping company's outstanding bills, but she would still have to secure a loan against future dividends to carry her for a few more months. It had taken a good deal of persuasion on Ryder's part to bring the loan officer at the Lyndon Point Community Bank to where the man was willing to go along with that option.

Ryder would help Aunt Myra with the loan application, and he would also help her restructure her company's financial picture. She was much better at designing intricate landscapes than figuring out profit-and-loss statements.

After a glance at his watch, Ryder pushed away from the desk. The aunts were having lunch at the Nest, and he'd agreed to join them to explain what he'd come up with for Aunt Myra. He was glad he had something challenging to occupy his mind. The last thing he wanted to think about was Lucie and her designs on Great-great-grandfather Percy's house.

He had yet to come up with a solution to that mess, even though after he went home in the evenings, he did little else but think about it. His problem stemmed from his divided loyalties. He didn't see how he could choose between his sister and his daughter.

And his…well, Lucie.

Even though he'd fought against it, he had to admit she was more appealing now than she'd been six years ago. For different reasons.

Lucie was as pretty as ever, but now there were depths to her that hadn't been there when they'd first met. The way she looked at Chloe, how she cared for their daughter, moved him and awakened feelings he'd never imagined he could experience. The thought that she'd borne his child. That just about undid him.

He knew that bond would link them forever.

But were there more bonds between them?

Ryder didn't dare dig too deeply for that answer, and he hated the nagging suspicion that he was well on his way to becoming an emotional coward.

With a disgusted sigh, he stood and grabbed the manila folder with the paperwork he had to take to Aunt Myra. Time to put aside all thoughts of Lucie. Time for lunch.

Fifteen minutes later, Ryder walked into the Nest, its bubbling activity a welcome break in his day. A chorus of greetings arose when he stepped inside, and it took him a long ten minutes to make his way down the aisle to the booth where his aunts were seated.

With Lucie.

He fought the impulse to turn tail and run.

What was she doing with Aunt Edna and Aunt Myra? Had the sisters set him up? He wouldn't put it past them. Each aunt had told him a number of times how much she wanted him married and settled with a nice girl. They also had a distressing habit of throwing him into embarrassing situations in their misguided efforts to marry him off.

He'd never needed them to cook up a romance for him.

He wasn't about to need their help now with Lucie.

Ryder came to a halt next to the three laughing women when he realized the only spot they'd left for him was by Lucie. Nothing about the scenario struck him as funny. On the contrary, the urge to bolt struck hard one more time.

He squared his shoulders. "Hello, ladies."

"Ryder!" Aunt Myra exclaimed from her corner of the booth.

Aunt Edna bounced up and threw her arms around him. "You're just in time to join us." She pointed across the table. "And there's room for you right by Lucie." She nudged him. "Go ahead. Take a seat, dear. Wait until you see what we've got planned."

Alarms sounded. "Planned?"

He sat as close to the edge as possible.

Lucie arched a brow but said nothing.

Aunt Myra pushed a yellow legal pad across the table. "Take a look, Ryder. I can't believe how fortunate I am to have met Lucie. She's given me all kinds of ideas for my business."

Ryder's eyes slid to Lucie's.

She didn't flinch at his glare, but rather shrugged. "To do my job as a fashion buyer in New York," she said, "I had to keep a close eye on marketing. What the public wanted guided my choices. There are definite ways to identify the products that will appeal to customers, and ways to offer those products to their greatest advantage. I thought I could give Myra some tips."

Out the corner of his eye, he saw Aunt Myra bob her head. A glance at Aunt Edna revealed her beaming expression.

Nothing made sense. "And this was lunch conversation?"

"Business-lunch conversation," Aunt Edna said, a knowing smile on her lips.

"A business lunch," he repeated.

"Of course, Ryder," Aunt Myra added. "My business is in trouble, Lucie is a successful businesswoman and she's offered to help me step up my revenue opportunities. I'd be stupid not to take her up on her offer."

He zeroed in on the successful businesswoman at his side. "Revenue opportunities?" When Lucie only shrugged again, he continued. "How do you propose to step them up?"

Lucie shifted. "I don't propose to step them up single-handedly. I plan to help Myra market her business so that her customers will be more likely than not to keep hiring her, even in this tough economy."

"Lucie has great ideas," Aunt Myra said. "And she's showing me how to work up a business plan—never really had one of those before. We're going to start by restructuring the budget, reevaluating personnel needs, comparing costs between competing suppliers, containing equipment costs and the effect of worker safety on company insurance bills."

Had he traveled to another universe instead of to the Nest?

Ryder had never heard his aunt talk like that. Usually she discussed the specifics of particular flowers or shrubs, the attack of ravenous insects or the benefits of mixing manure with topsoil. Obviously she was regurgitating what she'd been fed.

Before he could comment, Aunt Myra went on. Ryder had to rub his aching head. Finally, when his aunt began to outline a potential class on the benefits of composting, he knew something smelled, and it wasn't the rotting stuff people spread on their lawns. He turned to Lucie.

"Seeing how you're so full of these great ideas, where do you intend for my aunt to offer these classes?"

Lucie tipped up her chin. "Myra says she'll clean up her equipment storage barn. That shouldn't take much money, mostly elbow grease, and I've offered to help."

"In between teaching her and all her friends to quilt and knit, right?"

Lucie sputtered like a radiator in trouble, but before he could continue she leaned forward, her eyes shooting off sparks. She jabbed the legal pad with her index finger. "Get serious, Ryder. I'm trying to help your aunt come up with year-round income. The whole point is to make Sorensen Landscaping viable and profitable. Which it isn't now."

"What about—"

"It might be easier if I gave you a rundown of what I suggested to Myra," Lucie said. "She's going to offer more targeted services, starting with eco-conscious weed control, compost pile starts and maintenance, energy-efficient and sustainable landscaping, winterizing irrigation systems and reopening them in the spring, snow and ice removal—rare enough in this area, I know, but when it's needed, it should make her money—supplying firewood and commercial interiorscaping."

Ryder's head spun. Where had she come up with all that? Maybe she had done her homework. And her spiel didn't sound half bad. It seemed to make sense. Still…

"New services aren't going to do it if her clients can't afford her to begin with," he countered.

"I agree," Lucie answered. "And that's why we're going to work on a new fee structure."

Off she went discussing commercial customers, bidding techniques, the solicitation of government contracts and marketing methods.

Her machine-gun delivery told Ryder she'd been a success in the jungles of New York, and suddenly made him wonder if he had any idea what improving the bottom line of his aunt's business might really entail. He'd never even thought of anything along these lines.

As he reeled, Lucie expounded, only stopping to take a sip of her iced tea. "And I also plan to make full use of the internet," she added. "We're going to launch a Sorensen Landscaping website, and we'll link to every other site that makes sense and will let us. It's inexpensive and reaches practically everyone."

She talked about Aunt Myra's business with passion, commitment and enthusiasm. She sounded like Aunt Myra herself, only with an East Coast twist of professionalism. He nodded slowly.

"It can't hurt." He turned to his aunt. "With the financing options I've developed for you—you know, your interest dividend and a loan against future interest—"

"Ryder?" his aunt said, a thoughtful expression on her face. "I think it's best if we hold off on siphoning any more interest from the trust fund, and I'd rather not take out another loan. I want to try Lucie's ideas since they won't take much out-of-pocket expenses. If for some reason we don't succeed, well, then we can look into your options. But I think we've come up with the right solution for me."

Aunt Edna, who'd been unusually quiet, patted her sister's hand. "You have, dear. This is what you've been missing all these years—oh, no!" She waved away her comment. "*Lucie's* what you've been missing all these years."

A thought zinged through his head, leaving him breathless. *Maybe Lucie's what I've been missing, too.*

As the random concept bounced in his mind, Ryder swallowed hard, choked, coughed and wheezed before he shrank back into the leather booth. As he sipped water from the glass the alert and concerned waitress placed before him, he fought to keep from rolling the dewed glass over his hot cheeks and forehead.

Where had that insane idea come from? He didn't really feel his life had been lacking Lucie's presence these past six years, did he? *Had* his life been missing something all those years?

Well, he had missed his sister for the last three.

And he had missed knowing Chloe.

But Lucie?

No. Couldn't be.

He really had to do something about those rebellious ideas. He couldn't let his brain keep sprouting such weed-like thoughts—

Oh, good grief! The three women even had him thinking in vegetation terms.

"Ryder?"

He stood when he realized he hadn't heard a thing Aunt Edna had said. He was in trouble.

He cleared his throat. "Well, ladies. Since Aunt Myra's not going to need my help, I should head back to the office."

He hugged the aunts, and when he turned to say goodbye to Lucie, he caught a strange and momentary expression on her face. Unless he was mistaken, it had been a look of longing.

But for what? His embrace?

Knock it off. She wasn't longing for him. Not after all these years.

Was she?

Chapter Eleven

As Ryder walked away, the skies opened up with a misty drizzle. Two blocks from his office, he realized he hadn't eaten while at the diner. He wasn't even hungry anymore.

The whole time he walked, an occasional greeting from a constituent jolted him from his thoughts. But each time, when he resumed his trek, his mind returned to the moments he'd spent with the three women at the diner. What had happened back there?

Ryder picked up his pace. What had happened was that Aunt Myra had found a solution to her problem.

He knew he should be happy for her. And he was.

He guessed.

Even so, he couldn't stop a strange sense of deflation. Which made no sense. How could he feel let down when his aunt had done something proactive for herself?

Hadn't he wished multiple times she'd depend less on him? Now it looked as though she was headed in that direction, so why did he have a vague sense of loneliness swimming inside him? He felt as though he'd become unnecessary.

How crazy was that?

One thing Ryder did know—he didn't like how he felt.

He ran a hand down his face and picked up his pace. He was making no sense, and he'd always been a sensible man. His no-nonsense levelheadedness had made him a pillar of Lyndon Point—it got him elected mayor. He couldn't let himself get carried away with silly ideas like deflation.

Loneliness?

Hah! Not with his throng of relatives.

Unnecessary?

As if that were possible with all their messes to fix.

If not tomorrow, then in a couple of weeks Aunt Myra would be back at his office, ready to look at the financing package he'd put together. He doubted Lucie's suggestions would solve Sorensen Landscaping's business woes, and when they didn't Aunt Myra would be right back where she'd started—where they'd all started. Depending on him—just as his other relatives did.

Just as the town of Lyndon Point did.

Lucie's presence in town wouldn't change a thing.

In the morning, Lucie glanced out the window, and when she saw the overall grayness outside, she snuggled deeper into the sheets. Chloe hadn't wakened yet—she didn't hear the TV in the adjoining room.

This was their last day at the hotel. In a couple of hours, she'd check out, and she and Chloe would be on their way to the Quigleys' beautiful B & B at the far north corner of Lyndon Point. And then…

Then what?

Yesterday had been a satisfying day. She'd spent hours preparing for her lunch with Edna and Myra, and her efforts had paid off. The two sisters had been thrilled with her ideas. Now Myra had a concrete blueprint and was excited to implement Lucie's suggestions.

But what about her?

She still had no place to live, nowhere to open her shop and no intention of going back to New York.

What was she going to do?

Her gut told her Ryder was her one and only stumbling block. His refusals smelled of personal issues. Everyone else at that city council meeting had made it clear they wanted her store in the Victorian. But hearing her presentation hadn't moved Ryder one bit.

Lucie wasn't ready to give up. Not yet. Not without a fight.

She shuddered. Fighting Ryder hadn't featured in any of her plans. Not even in her wildest imaginations could she have imagined the position in which she found herself. From where she stood, changing Ryder's mind seemed impossible, since he wouldn't even hear her out.

Fortunately, when it came to the impossible, she knew the Lord was still in business. Scooting up to a sitting position against the padded headboard, she reached for her Bible and began reading where she'd left off the day before.

A short while later she closed God's word, thoughts rushing around her head. Although she'd read the book of Proverbs countless times over the years, a particular verse in the nineteenth chapter had hit her just right this time. It made her think of another verse, the one about a man preferring to live out on a rooftop rather than inside with an argumentative woman.

Maybe she'd be better off if she rethought the concept of fighting Ryder for the Victorian house. After all, the old cliché said one would attract more bees with honey than vinegar, and she knew bugs did prefer sweetness. Not that Ryder was a bug.

Still, she couldn't help but remember another cliché, this

one about a fly in the ointment. It described his attitude to perfection.

"Mama!"

With a groan, Lucie set aside thoughts of bees and honey, flies and ointment. And Ryder. "Coming, Chloe."

She did focus on moving the two of them to the B & B in Lyndon Point, and then on unpacking their belongings into the exquisite antique chests in their connecting rooms. Unfortunately, she failed to block all thoughts of Ryder, as seemed to be the case more often than not these days.

And that was why she and Chloe walked into his office at a quarter to five, a brimming basket of goodies in the backseat of her rental car.

She just prayed her latest great idea didn't leave her nursing an emotional bee sting.

"You've come to my office to invite me to a picnic."

Lucie shifted her weight from foot to foot. He didn't seem thrilled by the idea, and she began to feel like a fool, but she was so far into it that she couldn't turn around and run back to the B & B. "That's right."

Chloe dropped Lucie's hand and stepped farther into the office, a look of wonder on her face. It was an impressive room. "A picnic on the beach, Mr. Daddy."

He smiled at Chloe, then turned to Lucie. "On the beach."

"Of course."

Chloe skipped to one of the brimming bookshelves and ran a finger over the books' spines. "I'm gonna be a rock hound again. Wanna rock-hound with me?"

He nodded absently, his gaze on Lucie. "On a cloudy, gray afternoon when we're expecting more showers."

Before Lucie found an appropriate response, Chloe walked up to Ryder's large desk and peered over the edge.

"Hey, I'm hungry, and Mama bought us some good food." She giggled. "I didn't see a lot of green stuff, either."

Lucie smiled and tipped up her chin. "Look, Ryder. You should know better than me. This is the Pacific Northwest. You guys are known for living in a hazy, gray world. If I waited until I was sure we'd have a perfect day for a picnic, I've a feeling I'd be waiting until I turned as gray as today."

He tilted his head. "You do have a point there."

Okay. There was progress. "And you do have to eat— another point."

"Well taken."

Chloe clutched the edge of the desktop and did a little jig—she'd been looking forward to the picnic since Lucie had revealed her plans. "I hafta eat too, Mr. Daddy. Please come with us."

Lucie drew a breath for courage. "We still need to discuss our daughter's situation. I think you can see that spending time with her when we can talk undisturbed and in private—" she gave a nod toward Chloe "—relatively private, makes a lot of sense."

He pushed back from his desk and closed the file he'd been reading. "You like picnics, Chloe?"

"I looooove picnics, Mr. Daddy!"

"Then today we will have us a picnic."

Lucie's shoulders sagged in relief.

He turned to her. "Where exactly do you plan for us to have this picnic?" The silver pen he'd been using went into the black leather holder at the front of the desk, and he straightened the fat envelope at one of the corners a millimeter or two. "There's a whole lot of very rocky beach out there."

Before she could answer, he stood, picked up a stack of

papers from the other gleaming edge of the desk's surface, opened the door and nodded for her to go ahead.

When the man made up his mind, he made up his mind. Lucie slipped past him into the waiting room. "Mrs. Quigley suggested their own beach—it's beautiful out there. Since Chloe and I are the only guests at the B & B right now, we should have the privacy I suggested."

Chloe scooted in between them. "Oh, Mr. Daddy! I like Mrs. Wiggly. She's gonna take me to play. At the park. While Mama works on the weeds." Chloe turned to Lucie, a frown on her brow. "I want to play at the park, but I want the weeds, too."

He arched a brow at Lucie as he crossed to Wendy's desk.

She blushed, picked her words carefully. "Mrs. Quigley plans to take Chloe to a park to play with her grandchildren—"

"And ice cream!" Chloe said. "I looooove ice cream."

Lucie was glad for the distraction Chloe provided. She didn't want to touch the subject of the house. Not after what she'd arranged with Myra.

"I'm so fortunate to have heard about the Quigleys' B & B," Lucie said. "Mrs. Quigley is wonderful, and Chloe loves her. After the park, she'll take the kids downtown to the Creamery. Their ice cream is fabulous."

"The kids will enjoy that." He turned to his receptionist. "Here you go, Wendy. The Edmonds Auto Body and Service papers are ready for signatures. Please give them a call and set up an appointment for Art and Stu to come in."

Wendy's brows shot up behind the edge of the rimless glasses. "You're leaving? It's barely five o'clock. You never leave this early. Is something wrong, Boss?"

"It's okay, Wendy. Nothing's wrong. I just…um…" He

glanced at Chloe. "I have something more important to do today."

Wendy zeroed in on the woven-wood-slat picnic basket and its red-and-white-checked napkin cover. She gave Lucie and Chloe a once-over.

Lucie felt more out of place than an Eskimo in the Sahara. She slipped the basket behind her with one hand, then reached for Chloe with the other.

Wendy shot her an intrigued look before turning back to Ryder, a sly grin on her pixielike face. "Never known you to ditch your work for a picnic before. Gotta mean something, all right."

To Lucie's amazement, Ryder blushed. "Yeah, it does," he answered. "It means I'm hungry and Lu—Ms. Adams has gone to the trouble of preparing a picnic for us. I'm going with her." He looked at Chloe, deep tenderness on his face. "With her and someone very, very special. Wendy, this is Chloe...my...daughter."

Wendy's brown eyes opened to an almost humorous size. "Your daughter—for real, then? Like daughter... *daughter?*"

His brows met over the bridge of his nose. "Wendy. There's only one way to understand my statement. Chloe is a wonderful young lady, and I'm fortunate enough that she's my daughter. Now, we have a picnic scheduled. I'll see you tomorrow."

Lucie's discomfort grew as Wendy's gaze shot to her. While she wished she could avoid the woman's searing scrutiny, she eventually decided she had no reason to flinch, so she met Wendy's gaze full on.

Long moments later, Wendy donned a brilliant grin, and Lucie figured she must have passed some kind of test. "I'll close up, Boss. And I'll see *you* tomorrow. Bye, Lucie and Chloe."

Ryder's assistant spun her brown leather office chair around and went back to her computer, her fingers clicking rapid-fire rhythms against the keys.

Lucie couldn't remember when she'd ever been dismissed more thoroughly or cheerfully. While most assistants didn't treat their bosses like the woman had just done, Lucie knew Ryder was in for the real grilling tomorrow.

Ryder took hold of Lucie's elbow to lead her out of the office and folded his other hand around Chloe's little fingers. The warmth of his hand sent a ripple of awareness up Lucie's arm, and she wondered if he could tell how much his touch affected her.

A glance at Ryder revealed nothing. When he continued to hold her arm, her response to his nearness intensified. He matched his steps to hers, and she felt enveloped by his presence; she even sensed his breathing. Lucie couldn't remember if she'd responded this intensely to him when they first met.

Once outside, a fine mist fell around them, and a faint chill ran through Lucie. She shivered. Even though she knew the damp air had struck her, she didn't know if it had triggered her shiver or if Ryder was responsible for that.

She hoped she could blame the rain. If not, she was in deep, deep trouble.

"Are you cold?" he asked, drawing her closer to his side.

His protective gesture pleased her—against her better judgment. "N-no. Just…um…the damp. It caught me by surprise."

He smiled. "If you really plan to move out here, you're going to have to get used to it soon."

Lucie nodded, certain she'd adapt to the climate sooner than she'd learn to ignore the way his touch affected her.

"I like it, Mr. Daddy," Chloe said, skipping at Ryder's side.

Clearly charmed, Ryder focused on Chloe during the short walk to the parking lot. Lucie basked in the connection between father and child.

To her surprise, he didn't argue when she said she'd drive to the Quigleys' place, with him following behind. Once at the B & B, however, he took the basket and insisted on carrying it to the beach. Lucie didn't object. Since she hadn't known what he might like to eat, she'd gone for a wide assortment of choices when she'd shopped earlier that afternoon. The basket weighed a ton.

By the time they reached the tiki-style hut on the waterfront, the rain had stopped.

Lucie spread the tablecloth she'd packed in the basket over the wood plank floor, then laid out the many goodies she'd bought.

"Help yourself," she told Ryder as she prepared a plate of lean roast beef, fruit salad and baby carrots for Chloe. "I was thrilled by the variety I found downtown, even though Lyndon Point is such a small town."

Chloe sat at the edge of the structure and munched away. Lucie handed Ryder a plate, then began to serve herself.

He scooped out a generous portion of the multicolored veggie and pasta salad with a serving spoon she'd borrowed from Mrs. Quigley. "Small doesn't mean backward."

"I never meant that." She helped herself to the roast beef. "Is Lyndon Point taking advantage of all these pluses to draw tourism here?"

Ryder shrugged. "We get the overflow from Edmonds. The ferry to the Olympic Peninsula leaves from there and they have the marina. They've spent years building up those features of their town."

"Don't you think Lyndon Point would benefit from marketing its own unique features?"

He opened a chilled bottle of iced tea. "We don't have

a ferry terminal here, and that's what really puts Edmonds on the map."

They fell silent for a while as they enjoyed their meal, interrupting the peace only with occasional comments on the food, the stark beauty of the gray afternoon and even their hopes for Myra's business future. Mostly, though, they watched Chloe, who after eating had resumed her search for rocks.

"Don't get too close to the water," Lucie called. "You don't want to get wet."

"Your mama's right," Ryder said. "The water's very, very cold here. Maybe you should move away a little. There are more and bigger rocks a bit farther from the edge."

They went back to their food, and as they ate, they talked about the temperature, the endless gray of the day, the breeze and whether the predicted storm would indeed strike. Soon, though, they finished all they could eat and exhausted the small talk. That's when Lucie reached into the picnic basket one more time and pulled out a rectangular green book. She breathed a silent prayer for God's blessing upon her efforts, and then placed a hand on Ryder's forearm.

"I'd like you to have this," she said. "I put it together over the years, adding to it all the time. I always hoped I'd find you someday."

His obvious surprise made her voice falter, but she forged ahead. "Now that I've found you, I'm handing it over. The rest is up to you."

He hesitated to take the book she held out, and wariness darkened his expression. He met her gaze. "You've been here almost two weeks. What were you waiting for?"

She shrugged. "I think you'll understand why I had to take my time, to be sure of you, when you look through it."

The hard set of his jaw told her he didn't like her answer,

but it was the best he was going to get until he opened the book and looked from beginning to end.

He reached for the small tome. As he paged past the cover, Lucie again prayed. While she still had her eyes closed, she heard his sharp inhale, and she knew he'd seen the first photo.

Chloe, moments after birth, cradled in Lucie's arms.

Instead of looking at Ryder, she turned to gaze at the subject of the album, then out over the ocean, her soul forming additional, incoherent prayers for understanding, for appreciation, for Ryder's heart to swell with love as great as hers for their child. For hidden longings she didn't dare give voice.

When the silence had stretched longer than she could bear, Lucie stole a glance at him from the corner of her eyes.

Ryder's expression was undecipherable. What she could and did understand, though, was the powerful effect the photos of their daughter had on him. Raw emotion radiated from his stunning blue-gray eyes, which sparkled with the brilliance of unshed tears. In one hand he held the album, and with the fingers of the other, he caressed a close-up of Chloe. When he lifted his gaze to the child, bright in her pink outfit against the drab horizon, a tear rolled down his lean cheek.

That single, physical expression of his feelings hit Lucie hard. She'd known the Ryder of the past, the young college athlete, intelligent, tender, exciting, but seemingly uninterested in permanence. She also knew the successful businessman and local politician, a man who kept his office immaculate, and ran a town with the same efficient organization. A man who now seemed grounded, and as devoted to permanence as he'd shunned it before.

It was unfortunate that Lucie had come up against

the man who also seemed unmoved by her desire to do the right thing…for her as well as for Chloe. She had at least weighed the merits of a number of listings Edna had brought her. Unfortunately, even Edna agreed none would really work.

These newer facets of Ryder captured her attention, puzzled her, intrigued her. But this man, the one moved to tears by images of his child…this Ryder was far more dangerous than the others. This man added the best of the man who stole her heart years ago to the mature, settled Ryder, then took it all to a higher level altogether.

"Thanks," he said, a tremor in his voice.

He stood and slowly walked to Chloe's side. He dropped down to one knee, reached out and ran a finger down a rounded cheek.

Chloe placed her small hand on his lean cheek, smiled, rubbed it and let out a happy giggle.

This time, a tear rolled down Lucie's cheek.

This Ryder was the one who'd never left her thoughts for long. This Ryder had never vanished from her memories or from her heart. This Ryder still held her heart in his hands.

Lucie's breath caught in her throat. She'd done everything to avoid it, but she couldn't run from the truth any longer. That truth was crazy, unwise. Certainly dangerous to her future.

She couldn't even get Ryder to speak to her about the house she wanted to buy. Not in any meaningful way. So how could there ever be a future for them? Maybe the future was only a promise for Ryder and Chloe, for father and daughter. Lucie would have to take a step back, watch from a distance, salve her broken heart from far away.

Ryder had the power to hurt her. He had the power to break her heart again.

It was way past time to face facts. She still loved him, more now that she'd seen his response to Chloe's baby album.

She loved him, but...

Did he love her?

Chapter Twelve

The first photo of his daughter, clearly moments after her birth, was Ryder's undoing. It crushed his insides into a mass of feelings, feelings too unfamiliar to fully identify. He recognized the fear, sure. He didn't know a thing about being a father, so that made sense, and he knew he had to learn fast. But anxiety was the least of what he felt.

His heart seemed to have expanded in his chest. Something rich and deep and powerful stretched within him, filling him to where he didn't know if his body was going to contain it. He might just burst with that...what was it?

Pride?

Love?

Joy?

But how could he feel so much when he barely knew Chloe? Had God hardwired him to love his child way back when He created Ryder? Was that what parents always spoke of when they went on and on about their children?

Well, if that was it, then he got it. He finally got it.

If not before, then certainly when Chloe reached out and rubbed his evening-stubbled cheek as though she'd been doing it her whole life. His heart swelled with emotion, and it was all he could do to keep a whole flood of tears contained.

Ryder supposed his feelings would grow greater and deeper as he spent time with his little girl. Getting to know Chloe was going to be the greatest adventure he ever undertook. And he owed it all to Lucie.

In spite of all the difficulties she'd faced, in spite of her father's opposition, Lucie had cared so much that she'd met everything head-on in order to bear their child. That recognition added to the swarm of feelings in Ryder's heart. In spite of how much they disagreed over Great-great-grandfather Percy's place, she was quite a woman. A strong woman, a loving mother, one with a heart full of love.

She displayed a courage he couldn't help but admire. And appreciate. Lucie was a remarkable woman.

He looked over his shoulder. "Thanks," he said, his voice rough, unsteady.

Chloe was a fortunate little girl. While he hadn't been around these past six years, Lucie had been, and from all he could tell, she'd done a great job raising their child.

He fought to keep from snorting in self-disgust. Lucie, brave, strong, loving Lucie, had been willing to pull up roots and travel across the whole United States to do what she believed to be in Chloe's best interests. She'd done it not knowing how things would turn out for herself in the end.

That was love. Pure, unadulterated, mind-boggling love. Oh, yeah. Lucie Adams was one amazing lady.

And he'd pretty much been a jerk to her.

The enormity of her actions moved him, they humbled him. And left him wishing…wishing for more. Not just for his daughter, but for himself as well. He'd never known love that deep since his parents and grandparents died. And that had been different.

Then, as much as he'd loved his sister, Deanna, he doubted she'd ever felt the same love for him. Dee hadn't shown any qualms about leaving in spite of Ryder's concern and objections. She clearly hadn't cared much about him.

Certainly not in comparison to the love Lucie seemed capable of feeling. He wondered…had Lucie ever loved a man that much? If so, where was he now? If not, then why hadn't she?

Did he stand a chance to earn that love? Had he blown his chances six years ago? Or had he done that by acting like an idiot since she arrived in Lyndon Point?

Ryder drew in a ragged breath. He'd been skirting the truth since the day he saw her again. His world had just tilted after his gut-deep recognition of Chloe's place in his life. Ryder knew he was a fool if he tried to avoid reality any longer.

He'd always known he'd fallen hard for Lucie all those years before. Truth was, he'd never recovered from the impact of their brief, intense relationship.

Question was, did she know? Did she care?

What did she feel for him?

Had she only come out west for their daughter's sake?

Or could she possibly love him after all this time?

As he loved her.

Still.

Ryder returned to Lucie's side in the tiki hut. She waited for him to speak.

He didn't. Instead, he picked up the album again, stared at Chloe's picture, then covered it with his hand again.

Before she realized what she was doing, Lucie laced her fingers through Ryder's, right over the picture of their child. The gesture brought her closer to him, up against his side. The scent of some spicy cologne teased her nostrils, and his warmth again enveloped her.

Oh, yes. She still loved him. Just being next to Ryder did strange things to her common sense. Like right then. She felt an unseen tension pull her closer to him. No power she knew could have moved her away at that moment.

She looked up from where their hands lay on Chloe's image to check Ryder's reaction. He'd turned toward her, had leaned close to her. He was now only a breath away.

Lucie dragged her gaze from his broad chest to his strong neck, from his square chin, over his high cheekbones and straight nose up to where his blue-gray eyes stopped her. The two of them sat there in the tiki hut on the lonely beach, silent, studying each other, the bond between them holding them in its gentle grip.

Her heart pounded, hard and fast, and Lucie was afraid Ryder would hear it and know what he did to her emotions. But time seemed to have stopped. The only thing she registered was Ryder's nearness, his breath feathering against her lips, and the realization that if she moved a fraction of an inch, they'd touch, their lips would meet. If that were to happen, she didn't know how she'd react, how she'd respond—

Ryder covered her lips with his. Lucie melted into him, every bit of her remembering his touch and his caresses. She leaned into his strength and warmth, his tenderness willing her to respond in kind, to kiss him back with the same need, the same longing he seemed to express.

She'd missed this—she'd missed *him*.

After long, tender moments, he pulled away slowly, gently, his eyes studying her. His hand reached out to run his fingers through the length of her hair. They sat like that for long moments, and Lucie marveled at the intensity of her feelings for him. Who would have thought that time and distance would have done nothing to diminish what she'd once felt for him so long ago.

"Lucie—"

"Shh…" She covered his lips with her index finger, unwilling to break the fragile beauty of the moment. Because now she knew. She knew she'd been lying to herself all that time. It hadn't been only a college-kid infatuation, with life-altering consequences. Something inside her had recognized Ryder as a man she could love forever, and being the kind of woman she was, she'd done just that. She'd fallen in love for a lifetime.

Now they were together again.

She didn't know for how long or in what kind of relationship, but right then she didn't want to ruin the gossamer mood with those realities. Right then she wanted to love and thank God for this special time with the man she loved.

The man she knew she'd always love.

He seemed to understand her reluctance to break the spell, and merely wrapped his arm around her. With a contented sigh, she laid her head in the hollow of his shoulder. They sat like that, together, with the photo of their daughter before them, as Chloe continued to gather beach pebbles. Long, silent minutes went by.

Chloe's clattering footsteps on the steps of the tiki hut put an end to the moment. She held out both hands, the fingers curled around more rocks. "Look, Mr. Daddy! I got a big collection now."

"Sure looks that way. Can you count them? Can you tell me how many you have in your hands?"

Chloe dropped her handfuls of pebbles—not many, since her hands were small—then began to count. "One, two, *fff-free,* five, six—no! Let me start again.…"

After a couple of efforts, Lucie noticed her daughter's

eyelids drooping. Then Chloe stunned her. She gathered up her rocks again, looked from Lucie to Ryder, then scooted over to his side. As if it were the most natural thing to do, she crawled in his lap and placed her head on his chest.

She watched Ryder struggle with the emotions. With a deep sigh, he regained his composure as Chloe's breath grew slow and deep.

"Wow…" he said.

She smiled.

They again sat in silence a few moments, but after a while a question refused to go unanswered any longer.

When she couldn't mute it for another second, she turned to Ryder, cupped her hand over his hard jaw and turned him so that he met her gaze.

"Talk to me about the house," she said.

She feared he wasn't going to do as she'd requested, but after a minute she felt his nod before she saw it, and the tension in her shoulders eased a bit.

He nodded again. "Okay. I guess I owe you that much. But it's not going to be easy. It'll take me more than a quick few words."

"That's fine. Chloe will sleep a bit longer, and I'm currently unemployed, so there's no work waiting for me in my room. There's nowhere else I have to be. Take all the time you want—or need."

Lucie heard the emotion vibrate in Ryder's voice when he told her about his parents, his grandparents and his younger sister, Deanna—Dee, as he called her. He described the accident that took his parents' lives and about the negligent repairman whose carelessness left Ryder to care for his younger sister earlier than he was ready to do so.

When Ryder seemed to run out of steam, Lucie waited,

giving him the time to compose himself instead of asking for more details.

As the setting sun painted the gray cloud fringe on the verge of the horizon with a ripe-persimmon tint, Lucie breathed yet another prayer for courage and for the right words to best give voice to her question.

"I understand your love for your family, Ryder, and I envy you the closeness you shared. I'm also sorry for your losses." She paused for another breath, seeking the assurance she needed to delve for the answers she'd wanted since she'd come to town. "But Ryder, I don't understand. I thought you were going to tell me about the house. What's the connection between your parents, grandparents and sister and the house?"

Ryder let out a gusty breath, shook his head, and Lucie felt his tension radiate toward her. He closed the photo album before he turned to Lucie. "My great-great-grandfather, Percy Augustus Lyndon, built that house for his bride, Eliza. It was the family home for years, but in the late twenties, his finances crashed with the country's economy. He had to sell. It hit them hard, especially Eliza, and both lived with that regret until their deaths."

While the tale so far was a sad one, Lucie knew it wasn't the whole story. She forced herself to be patient and give Ryder the time to tell it his way. But she remained ready to prod him again if needed. *She* needed the whole story, since it was the stumbling block to her future.

In a rusty voice, Ryder continued. "About six or seven different owners came and went over the years, and the house became a funeral parlor, a bridal store, offices and a bunch of other different things. Since the time Dee was a little girl, she loved the house and its connection to the family. Growing up, she talked all the time about the house and how she was going to buy it, fix it up and live in it with her family until the time she had to move to a nursing home."

Lucie sucked in a breath. *Uh-oh.* She didn't like the direction this was taking.

Chloe murmured and wriggled in Ryder's lap. He eased his hold on her, let her settle into a more comfortable position.

He smiled.

The dread in Lucie's gut lessened for a moment.

He picked up the thread of his story. "One year, instead of begging for Disney, Dee talked Aunt Edna and me into taking her to San Francisco to see their famous 'Painted Lady' Victorians."

The smile on his lips turned sad, but only for a moment. His expression immediately went blank, followed by a hint of anger in the tightness of his jaw, the narrowing of his eyes. "Three years ago, Dee was studying art at the University of Washington, and her love for historical properties had grown into a passion."

Lucie's stomach dropped to her toes. Things looked worse with everything he said.

"Ryder—"

"Hang on," he said. "I told you it wasn't a couple-of-words kind of story. It's not easy for me to talk about this."

He turned toward the sunset, his voice dropping to a husky murmur. "Dee fell for some artist bum who rode into town on his Harley, with little more than canvases and paints to his name. She dropped out of school and decided she needed to 'see the world' more than she needed an education. She said her art wouldn't mature in school, but that by—" his tone turned mocking "—'following her bliss' she'd gain the depth she needed to take the next step in her career. We argued, over and over again. I said things I never should have thought, much less yelled, at my sister."

Ryder's voice shook and he ran a hand through his hair. "What can I say? I lost control of my temper, went with my anger and fear. I let myself go with my impulses instead of thinking things through, carefully choosing my words, appealing to Dee's common sense. I blew it. And she's gone. I failed my parents and grandparents. Dee, too."

Something wasn't right. "Why haven't you called or visited her? Why haven't you told her what you've told me? I'm sure she would hear you out and accept your apology. I'm sure she loves you and wants to repair—"

"I'd give anything to be able to do that." His fervor told Lucie he truly meant what he said. "But over the years I've done everything to find her, with no result. I hired two different investigators. One of them went through income tax records and all that kind of thing. Nothing. They found no trace of her. I—I don't even know if…if she's—"

"Hush!" she said, reaching for his shoulder, all she could reach without jostling Chloe. "Don't even think that. If you haven't heard anything, neither good nor bad, don't torture yourself with the bad. These days it's supposed to be fairly easy for a person to disappear. And unless they break the law, it's tough to find them."

Ryder glanced over her way. "How do you know about that kind of thing?"

Lucie sat straighter. "I watch TV, you know."

To her relief, he chuckled. "That's called *fiction,* Lucie. You can't go by what you see on TV."

"It's called the news, Ryder. I'm a cable news junkie. I flip from news channel to news channel so I can soak up all sides of a story. I like to make up my mind myself. And that's what I've learned about people who want to disappear."

"A news junkie, huh?"

"That's me."

"You might be right. She's probably hiding. And she's stubborn. It might take the shifting of the moon and stars for her to admit a mistake."

She scooted closer, leaned toward him again. "I can see where you've had a rough time with all your family problems, but from what you've told me, none of them ever lived in that house, right? I don't get your position. If you want it, why haven't you bought it?"

He stiffened but didn't turn to face her, stared toward the sound, their daughter asleep in his arms. "Because it's my sister's dream, not mine. I failed to keep her safe, here where our family lives, where she'd have all the love and support she could ever need. Sooner or later Dee's reckless choices will lead to failure, and that's when she'll come back to Lyndon Point. I want her to find the house, ready and waiting for her. I want to help *her* buy it so she can fulfill her dream. I want her to be able to restore it, to bring it back to what it was when Percy and Eliza lived in it. I can't fail Dee again."

Lucie sagged. Well, at least now she knew the reason behind his vehemence. It didn't make a whole lot of sense, since it seemed obvious that if the adult Dee had still wanted the house, she would have come home by now.

But from the tension still in Ryder's shoulders, she knew this wasn't the time to debate the merits of his reasoning. While her savings weren't endless, she had enough to hold off on pressuring Ryder for a while. She could give him a few days to process what he'd told her. From the way he'd spoken, it sounded as if he'd never put his feelings into words before, as if he'd just poured them out. Maybe the telling would work as a catharsis. Maybe he'd see the flaw in his thinking.

Reading between the lines of what Ryder had just said, Lucie didn't think Dee's actions were those of a woman who dreamt of owning the house. Wouldn't she have come back to Lyndon Point by now if she'd been that committed to it? If his sister no longer wanted to live in Lyndon Point and restore the place, then it didn't matter how long Ryder kept it empty. Sooner or later he would have to relinquish his hold on the place.

It made sense for him to come to an agreement with City Council and her. Then Lucie could start to bring the lovely old home back to its previous beauty.

Sooner rather than later.

But this wasn't the time to argue. All she said was, "I understand."

To her surprise, he turned a fraction to face her. He leaned over their daughter to place a gentle kiss on Lucie's lips. When he pulled away, she wanted to draw him back to her, to feel his warmth again, to revel in the feelings his kiss evoked.

"Mmm," Chloe said, rubbing her eyes. "I want a kiss, too, Mr. Daddy. Hug and kiss, please?"

As Ryder hugged Chloe close and tickled her with his evening-stubbled chin, Lucie gathered up the remains of their picnic. It was getting late. She really had to get Chloe to bed. And the moment between her and Ryder had passed.

The little girl gave her daddy a good-night hug, then took the hand Lucie extended.

"We'll talk some more, right?" she asked Ryder as she started toward the handful of weather-beaten steps from the beach up to the Quigleys' backyard.

He clearly struggled with an answer, as his taut jaw and stiff shoulders revealed. But instead of replying, he gripped the photo album in one hand, and with the other pushed himself up from where he'd sat. He gave Lucie a long look, turned, then headed for the steps. At the bottom rung, he paused.

"Thanks for the album. It means the world." He swallowed hard.

"I—I'll be in touch. To set something up for me to spend more time with Chloe."

His footsteps rang out sharp against the seasoned wood.

Lucie stayed by the tiki hut, the sky growing darker as she stood, emotionally drained, suspecting he was in worse shape. She wished she could comfort him. But she didn't have the right.

Would she ever earn that right?

Would he ever see the subject of the Victorian from her angle?

Maybe sharing the details of his family situation hadn't been cathartic, as she'd first thought. Maybe, because of his many losses, Ryder had become too rigid over time, too boxed in to some exaggerated concept of self-control. Maybe he would never yield.

What would she do then?

Chapter Thirteen

"Good morning!" Mrs. Quigley said two days later, as she stirred something savory-scented in a deep pot on the stove. "Is my little darling still sleeping? I hope nothing's wrong with her."

Lucie crossed the immaculate blue-and-white kitchen to pour herself a generous mug of coffee from the coffee-maker on the marble counter. "On the contrary. Chloe was up late telling me all about her afternoon with you and your grandkids. I can't thank you enough for taking her to meet them. She had a great time."

Chloe's playtime with the Quigley kids had afforded Lucie and Ryder an opportunity to meet so they could discuss a schedule for Chloe and Ryder's time together. They'd focused solely on Chloe, and Lucie thought Ryder seemed as awkward and hesitant as she felt.

"I do appreciate the time you've spent with Chloe," she told him.

Lucie's short, plump hostess waved her wooden spoon. "Oh, pshaw! That sweetheart stole my heart the minute she walked in here. And kids are kids. They need to play. I'll be happy to take her to visit my grandkids anytime you want. That way you can see to..." She gestured in a circular motion. "You can take care of any business you might have. And like I told you yesterday, if you trust me, I'd love to keep Chloe rather than you having to put her in daycare. We'd have so much fun, and we can work something out that'll go very easy on your finances."

At the table, Lucie helped herself to a fragrant golden muffin studded with cranberries. She set down the coffee, pulled out a chair, then took a seat. She'd found the perfect person to watch Chloe, so technically Lucie could go to work, but she hadn't been able to put together the store just yet.

If Ryder didn't relent, she might never be able to do so.

Even though Edna Lyndon had continued to look into properties for Lucie, and she'd even toured a couple, so far nothing even remotely possible had come on the market. Great-great-grandfather Percy's Victorian was still the perfect place for Lucie and Chloe.

"Are you okay, honey?"

Lucie looked up to find Mrs. Quigley at her side, worry etched in the tiny lines around her eyes, the V between her brows, the twin creases across her forehead.

She shrugged. "I'm fine. It's just that my plans aren't going anywhere. I'm frustrated, and I can't help but think I may have misunderstood what I thought was God's leading. I may have made a mistake coming to Lyndon Point with the thought of trying to open a shop here."

Mrs. Quigley sat across from Lucie, her cup of tea in front of her. "Why don't you tell me how you came to choose Lyndon Point?"

Lucie met Mrs. Quigley's kind gaze. "I came to Lyndon Point because this is where Ryder Lyndon lives."

The older woman nodded, the pure white braid she coiled around her head gleaming like ivory in the sunlight that poured through the kitchen window. "It was the right thing to do, honey. I hope that's not why you regret your move. The two of them need each other."

Lucie choked, coughed and eased the burn in her throat with another sip of coffee. "You know, too? It's all over town already, isn't it?"

"Oh, dear me, yes. Your little Chloe looks just like Dee Lyndon when she was that age. Dee and Ryder always shared that strong family resemblance. One can't look at your baby's eyes and not see her daddy in them."

Lucie wrapped both hands around her mug and shrugged. "The relationship back then, a college spring-break fling, was a mistake, but Chloe isn't. She's the main reason I do anything from day to day. And you're right. She needs her father, just as Ryder needs his child. It's just…"

After a few minutes, Mrs. Quigley said, "It's just what?"

"It's just that Ryder is standing in my way. I want to open a fabric arts store—"

"We're all excited about it. Can't wait to see what goodies you're going to sell us."

"You might have to wait a long time." Lucie curved her lips in a wry grin. "Ryder won't even talk about the possibility of letting me buy the house from the city. He never told me his reasons until we had the picnic the day before yesterday. Now…"

She pushed her chair away from the table and began to pace. "It's not even a good reason. To me, he sounds confused, and from my point of view, he's looking at the situation the wrong way."

Mrs. Quigley tsk-tsked. "I can imagine. That boy's been punishing himself over Deanna's decision this whole time. I thought he was getting better. You know. Moving past it. But I guess all he's done is get better at hiding his feelings."

A thought occurred to Lucie. "Does everyone in town know all about this?"

"Some do, but I'm a good friend of Edna and Myra. We've talked about Ryder many times."

"So you understand where I'm coming from."

The white braid gently bobbed back and forth with her nod. "I understand. And I also understand where he's—as you say—coming from. What I'm not sure about is what we can do to put all this to rights."

"We?"

"Edna, Myra and me."

"Now that it affects Chloe and me, don't count me out of that group."

"Wouldn't think of it for a minute! I think you're just the breath of fresh air that boy needs. And Edna and Myra are crazy about you, too. You can count on us, dear. For anything."

It felt strange to know she wasn't totally alone—good, but strange. Lucie had been on her own for so long, she almost didn't know what it was like to have that kind of encouragement and respect. To have it come from three virtual strangers, three women who'd known Ryder all his life...

"Ryder seems fixated on Deanna's childhood dream," she said. "How does he even know, now that she's a grown woman, that it's still her dream?"

"The thought has occurred to me—to the three of us."

Lucie picked up steam. "Don't you think she would have made an effort to come back if the house still meant that much to her? That's what I would have done in her place."

"I wouldn't doubt it."

Lucie waved in a gesture of frustration. It all seemed crystal clear to her. "I'm afraid the only thing that might change his way of thinking is if he hears from Dee whether the house still matters to her as much as it once did."

"All that sounds logical," Mrs. Quigley said gently, "and you're probably right. But the only thing that matters is what Ryder thinks."

In the silence that followed, Lucie resumed pacing. She went from the back door, with its sparkly clean glass upper half, to the apron-front, country-style sink beneath the window, back and forth, over and over again. Mrs. Quigley didn't speak, and when Lucie glanced at her hostess, she had the impression the older woman was praying.

She was so glad she'd moved in. The Quigleys' B & B was proving to be the blessing she and Chloe had needed. That Mrs. Quigley, a prayer warrior of long standing, wanted to support Lucie in her endeavors, was just another of those special, unexpected gifts God gave His children. After all, the situation needed all the prayers they could muster.

As Lucie paused by the back door, an idea teased the furthest corners of her mind. It grew moment by moment, and took clearer shape as she gave it time.

The notion firmly in her sights, Lucie spun on her heel. "That's it, Mrs. Quigley. I know what I have to do. I have to find Deanna. That's the only way Ryder's going to be able to face his issues. I also think…"

How to put her vague but growing certainty into words? Lucie took a deep breath and went for it. "I think he's still hurting from his parents' and grandparents' deaths. He's told me how much he regrets the nasty confrontations with Deanna. I think he's holding on to that dream of hers as a way to cling to his last chance to make right whatever he still can. Does that sound too crazy?"

Mrs. Quigley, the epitome of discretion, only gave her a smile.

Lucie fumbled around for the best way to continue, then figured since she'd blundered along that far, she might as well just spit out her jumbled thoughts. "I don't think Ryder will ever be able to step into his future until he puts his past to rest. And Dee's his only tangible link to the past."

"People who are hurting see life along narrow lines."

"I know, I know. And it matters to me that Ryder's hurting. Because of Chloe. You know?"

Mrs. Quigley smiled again, this time with more humor than before.

Lucie refused to consider the reason behind the humor. She held out one hand, palm up. "Chloe needs her daddy." She flipped her other hand the same way. "Ryder needs to heal. For that, he needs to broaden his view of life. And the only way he's going to do it is by talking to Dee."

Her hostess didn't comment. Lucie went on. "Since he hasn't found her, I'm going to have to take up the reins of the search. I'm just going to do whatever I can to help him heal."

Mrs. Quigley's hazel eyes met Lucie's gaze. "Now, honey…how do you plan to do that? I know that boy's spent a bundle trying to locate Dee. What makes you think you can find her when he has failed?"

"I'm not sure I can find her, but I have to try. I can't give up. Chloe and I belong here in Lyndon Point. I know it's wrong to keep her and Ryder apart any longer, but I also need a way to earn a living." She tucked a lock of hair behind her ear and paced again. "Sure. I could open up a store just about anywhere. Then we'd have to shuffle Chloe from point A to point B all the time. She'd spend the better part of her days in a car. Even with the constant driving, we have to face reality. Ryder's a busy man, and once I find a place for my store, I'm going to be just as busy, if not more. How would a store in another town benefit the two of them?"

"I'm not arguing with your logic." Mrs. Quigley stood and nestled her mug in the dishwasher's top rack. "I'm just pointing out a hurdle."

"Let me think about it." It was going to take more than thought. It was going to take courage and humility on her part, but she wasn't ready to share her personal issues with Mrs. Quigley. Not yet. "I'm…pretty sure I can come up with something. One thing is certain. I can't sit back and waste any more time."

"I'll take up the prayer end of the project with Myra and Edna. Oh, and I'll watch Chloe for you whenever you want."

"Thanks. I appreciate both."

"Let me go call the sisters. We make quite a prayer team, if I do say so myself."

Now that Lucie had given voice to her idea, the niggling unease she'd been trying to ignore pushed its way forward. Sure, this was the right way to proceed, and she knew what her first step in the process had to be. But it was one step she wasn't eager to take.

She'd left the East Coast mainly to find Ryder, to introduce him and Chloe, but she'd also had another reason for leaving. One she didn't want to face, one which looked to be steaming toward her like a semi with defective brakes.

Lucie was going to have to reach out to her father, the father who'd always found fault with her behavior. While he'd never forgiven the bad decisions she'd made, neither had he praised the good ones. She was going to have to approach the man whose influence she'd had to escape to raise her daughter with the flexibility and freedom Chloe needed.

She had to call her father, and soon. As a renowned criminal attorney, Carter Adams had valuable contacts all over the country. If anything or anyone had harmed Deanna Lyndon, Lucie's father would know how to find out. There was a good chance his contacts would find her if she'd simply found a means to disappear. And they'd do it in a minimal amount of time.

Not only did her father have investigative connections all over the country, but he also had a personal interest in emerging artistic talent. He would know where to look for a budding artist like Deanna Lyndon.

Unfortunately, reaching out to him meant Lucie would again give Carter Adams access to Chloe. Not just that, but he would soon exert his considerable pressure on his daughter again.

"Lucie?"

The tension in her shoulders, neck and gut eased a fraction when she heard the tremor in the commanding bass voice.

"It's me, Dad," she said.

A relieved breath whooshed over the line. Then a cough to clear his throat. "I'm relieved you called, Lucinda. We were frantic, your brothers and I. You didn't leave us an address, and you haven't answered your phone since you disappeared. You know we've called dozens of times. How could you do that?"

Lucie fought the guilt his words poured over her. She shouldn't have refused to speak to her father and brothers, but she'd needed the distance to get her feet planted in her new world. She would never have been able to make any decisions with the three Adams men lobbying for her return to Connecticut, insisting she obediently follow their directions.

She'd told them she planned to move, but they hadn't wanted to hear her reasons. They had only argued, they'd done everything they could to dash her dreams.

"I'm sorry, Dad. It was the only way. We talked and talked, but you refused to acknowledge my point of view. I need to stand on my own, for myself and for Chloe."

"But we only want the best for you—"

"You need to accept that I can recognize what's best for me. And for Chloe."

"Your track record—"

"My one major lapse is in the distant past, where it needs to stay. But that's not why I called." Lucie pushed her hair off her forehead, too familiar with the arguments her father was about to make. "I need your legal expertise."

"You haven't been gone a month and you're already in trouble?"

She counted to ten. "No. I need to find someone, and if anyone can do it, you're the one."

"So you're finally ready to go after Chloe's father."

Time to talk, to tear the veil from that secret. "I already have. Ryder's the main reason I moved across the country, so that he and Chloe could build the relationship they should always have had."

A scoff exploded in her ear. "If I'm so good at finding missing persons, why on earth didn't you let me find that bum—that Ryder fellow—before now?"

"Can we talk about it another time? I really do need your help. It's urgent."

Her father's silence grew, and Lucie knew he was looking for his best negotiating stance. Before he could find one, Lucie went on. "Chloe's father has been trying to find his younger sister, Deanna, since she left their hometown about three years ago. He's done his best, but hasn't found a trace. I know you and your guys can do better. Will you help us?"

"Us, huh?"

Lucie drew in a sharp breath. "It—it's not like that, Dad." But a part of her wished it was. "We're not… 'together,' but I need to find her for a practical, business reason. And Ryder does need to know if his sister is all right."

Another silent debate on her father's end followed. The old-fashioned clock on the antique dresser in Lucie's room ticked the seconds away.

When Lucie thought she couldn't stand the tension another moment, he grunted, "Okay, but I'm going to need all the information you have. You and Chloe's…father."

Quickly, she told her father everything she'd learned about Dee Lyndon, about her interrupted college career, about her artistic talent, her love of vintage homes and her romance with the nomadic painter.

"Do you think you can find her?" she asked at the end of what she knew.

"That's not a lot to go on, but over the years Roger Miles has found plenty of reluctant witnesses for me with about as much. Let's give him a chance."

Lucie released the breath she'd been holding. "Thanks, Dad. Your help means more than I can put into words."

A pause. "As does your phone call to me. Thanks for your trust, Lucie. And…ah…I'm going to try and bite my tongue more often, okay?"

His offer stunned her. Hope in her heart, she said, "Thanks again. I have to go now, but I promise I won't let your calls go straight to voice mail anymore. Not unless I'm in a meeting or something. In that case, I'll call you back."

"I appreciate that."

A glance at the clock told her she had to retrieve Chloe. Mrs. Quigley had taken the child with her to the grocery store, but they'd probably returned already.

"I'll be waiting for the info, Dad. I—I love you."

In a rough, hesitant voice, he said, "Love you, too."

After she hung up, Lucie sat for a moment, absorbing the magnitude of what had just happened. Had she and her father reached a truce? Had her vanishing act had the effect she'd hoped and prayed for?

Only time, and Dad's actions, would tell.

Chapter Fourteen

Three days later, Lucie sat with Myra Sorenson in a patch of just-cleared earth on the overgrown grounds of Ryder's great-great-grandfather Percy's house, a stack of printouts between the two women.

Myra tapped the drawings with a dirt-stained finger. "That's where the original rose garden once was. I don't see any reason to move it elsewhere—"

"What is this?" Ryder said right behind them. "What are the two of you doing here?"

Uh-oh! Lucie had wondered how long it would take him to find her out. "I hired Myra, and we're discussing the restoration of the garden."

"You did what?" he roared. "What restoration? Last time I checked, you didn't own the place."

Lucie tipped up her chin. "Yet." She called on all her courage. "I've decided to make a donation to my new hometown. I'm donating the restoration so as to eliminate an eyesore from the center of Lyndon Point. Any problem with donations, Mr. Mayor?"

As Ryder sputtered some more, Myra rolled up her plans. "Uh—it sure looks like thunderclouds are incoming. Time to take cover."

Lucie glanced at the sky, but all she saw was clear blue. "Fine, fine. I'll see you later."

As Myra left, she turned back to Ryder, who was clearly gearing up to explode. Again. She cut him off before he could start. "Care to tell me why you didn't help your aunt by hiring her to maintain this place? She could have used the money, and the property could have used her expertise. Or is the eyesore a way to remind yourself that you're human and you made a mistake?"

"You're still trespassing," he bit off.

"And I'm still interested in buying this property. I'd just as soon start working on it before it gets any worse. Until I finalize the purchase, my donation gives the town a boost. Or are you going to reject my offer? City Council might object."

Lucie could see that Ryder wanted to react, to argue, but he drew himself up to his full height, his self-control evident in every line of his posture. He turned around and strode down the street, his steps long and forceful, but with none of the easy grace she'd noticed before.

She sighed. She might have won the momentary battle, but she wondered who would win the war.

She also hoped Chloe wouldn't be the lone casualty.

In the days that followed, Lucie didn't see Ryder even once. She knew he'd spent time with Chloe, even though he'd timed his arrivals at the B & B for those times when Lucie wasn't there. Mrs. Quigley always called when he arrived, making sure she knew he wanted to take their daughter on an outing. Lucie never refused his request, as certain as ever that whatever time they spent together was only to Chloe's benefit.

But she missed him. In spite of all her efforts otherwise. At first, she hadn't wanted to admit it, but she felt bad about the way they'd parted that last time. Still, she didn't think she'd done anything wrong by offering Myra much needed work that would expose the landscaper's talents to any number of future clients. Lucie had also gone ahead and checked into the town's requirements for donations and learned that as long as there were no strings attached, practically anything would be graciously accepted.

On another front, Lucie had yet to hear from her dad. She couldn't stand the feeling that she was in a holding pattern.

She still wanted the house for her shop. Ryder still wanted to keep the house a shrine to his pain. He still needed to face his past if he was ever to heal.

If there was to be any repeat of the closeness and kisses they'd shared on the beach.

Later that week, Lucie met Troy Sorensen, Myra's son, at the house. When the young man had learned how Lucie was helping his mother, he'd asked to speak to her about his stagnated business. It turned out he was a general contractor, and in the sluggish economy, his jobs had dried up to a scant trickle. He'd turned to Lucie for suggestions along the same lines as the ones she'd given his mother.

She'd come up with a list of ideas. And a proposition of her own.

"Thanks again for thinking of me," Troy said as Lucie studied the crisp, clear drawings he'd handed her. "I can't wait to get to work on this gorgeous house. I'd much rather do restoration work than remodeling, additions or high-end, luxury bath installations."

She smiled. "I'm looking to the future. And the less there is to repair at that time will only mean an earlier launch of my store."

"You're sure you like what I drew up for you?"

"What's not to like about new turned spindles, repaired and replaced gingerbread trim, and refastened fish-scale shingles on the turret?"

He chuckled. "Don't forget the termite-free boards for the porch!"

Lucie laughed.

That's when Ryder walked onto the grounds, his long legs parting the weeds like a miniature green version of Moses's Red Sea. Her heart leaped at the sight of him, but she forced a neutral expression on her face and tried to appear relaxed. The only time she'd seen him since their kisses on the beach was when he'd found her and Myra working on the garden.

Lucie had no idea where she stood with him. She hated the uncertainty.

His frown spoke volumes. Unfortunately, it didn't say anything all that great.

"What's that about shingles and boards?" he asked. "You're trespassing, Lucie. Yet again. It's becoming an issue."

Lucie handed the papers to Troy, who seemed determined to fade into the weeds.

"Are you going to call the police?" she asked. When he didn't respond, she tipped up her chin. "I'll have you know, I looked into abandoned-property code regulations. Since this house falls within the official description of an abandoned property, I filed a compliance complaint and am waiting to hear back on that. I also drew up documents to make a charitable donation—beautified grounds and restored exterior—to my new hometown. I'm giving Lyndon Point an attractive, well-landscaped corner to replace the sight that has up to now been a disgrace to the town. I don't think City Council will reject my gift. Especially since I hear Troy does exceptional work."

"Ah…" Troy said, backing toward the fence. "That's my cue to leave. See ya, Ryder, Lucie. Thanks!"

"Lucie," Ryder said, "You can't just go around—"

"Hi, Mr. Daddy," Chloe said as she rounded the corner of the house where Lucie had told her to play. "Wanna help me with the weeds?"

His lips thinned as he pressed them tight. "No, Chloe. I'd rather not. I need to talk to your mother."

Lucie crossed her arms. "Go ahead."

"I'd rather find neutral ground." He glanced at his watch. "It's almost time for lunch. Have any plans?"

"I mentioned the possibility of trying Tony's Pizzeria to Chloe earlier today."

"Excellent." He held out a hand to their little girl. "Let's go for that pizza."

They walked across Main Street and down a side road lined with more attractive businesses. While Lucie kept quiet, Chloe kept up a constant chatter as they went.

Tony's Pizzeria turned out to be a generous-sized eatery, its walls covered with murals of the Mediterranean countryside, cheerful Italian music overhead and the mouthwatering scent of herbs and spices in the air. Ryder led the way to the right side of the room, to a rectangular table for four draped in classic red-and-white-checked cotton. Chloe sat next to her father, which left Lucie to sit alone on the other side.

"Pep 'n ronni, please," Chloe said before they looked at menus.

Her father grinned. "Perfect. That's my favorite, too." His smile faded, however, when he turned to Lucie. "Okay with you?"

"Of course."

A teenaged boy with a stud through an eyebrow came to take their order. He scribbled on his pad, then handed

Chloe a children's paper place mat and a cup filled with crayons. When the boy left and Chloe busied herself with her artwork, Ryder turned to Lucie again, his eyes narrowed. "You're stubborn. And devious."

She lifted her chin a notch. "I prefer to think of it as determined and resourceful. Nothing devious about it. I told you I wanted to purchase the property. You refused to even discuss the matter. When it comes to stubborn, you have no room to talk."

"But I did talk. On the beach. I thought you'd respect my position after that."

Lucie let out a soft sigh. "I do understand where you're coming from, Ryder. But hasn't it occurred to you that your sister might not want the house anymore? Think about that tattered turret and sagging porch. Don't you think she would have come back to care for it if that were still her dream?"

He wouldn't meet her gaze, but instead drew designs with a short-trimmed fingernail on the bright tablecloth. "I think Dee's afraid to come back, after all I said to her. Some of our relatives were tough on her, too."

Lucie leaned forward. "I don't know. I'm a woman, too. If she's as strong-willed as I suspect she is, I think she'd be relentless in going after what she wants. I did—I'm still going after my dream." Compassion rising, she placed a hand on his arm. "What if her dream three years ago was one of freedom? What if she felt she had to leave to go after it?"

A muscle worked in his cheek, but he didn't speak.

She took a leap of faith. "Let me tell you a story—a family story."

Ryder didn't interrupt as Lucie described her father and two older brothers, and how she'd always felt belittled and smothered. How what they considered caring had felt anything but. She finished her tale by revealing her second reason behind the move west. "Believe me. It wasn't easy, but for my sake, and Chloe's, I had to escape."

He looked up, a hard glitter in his icy stare. "You know nothing about what happened between our family and Dee. She was swayed by her bum of a boyfriend. She'd never have left like she did if he hadn't pressured her."

"Are you sure he had to pressure her? Isn't it possible she might have chosen freedom over—oh, I don't know— your plans for her? Your expectations? Do you think she might have felt like she was stuck in a cage your brotherly love built around her as long as she lived here?"

Rage returned to his eyes. He sat taller, rigid, hands fisted, jaw squared. "You know nothing about Dee, Lucie. You've never even met her."

"You're right, I haven't. But I've been watching you, and what I've seen suggests your need to control might be behind Dee's disappearance."

Outrage colored his cheekbones a deep red. "Need to control? How can you try and twist my love for my sister into something she had to escape? I didn't do anything a brother who was left to care for his younger sibling wouldn't do."

"That's what you say today, now that I'm questioning your actions. It's not what you said on the beach the other night. In the dark your words implied that you might bear some guilt in her disappearance because you fought her so hard on her dreams, the path she wanted to pursue. You did say you recognized your share of responsibility in the situation."

Her words seemed to hit him as hard as a blow to his middle would have. He flinched. "I can't believe you're using against me my willingness to share something private and painful."

"I'm not using anything against you. I'm just repeating what you said, but in my own words. I think your rigid attitude has more than a bit to do with your own guilt."

"Shh!" Chloe held a finger to her lips. "We always use our nice voice, right, Mama?"

Lucie froze. What was she doing, fighting with Chloe's father right in front of her? No matter how much they disagreed, they didn't have to air the disagreement in front of their daughter.

"You're right, peanut." She gave Ryder a meaningful look. "Your father and I will use our nice voices from now on."

While she couldn't decipher the expression on Ryder's face, she easily read the softening of his lips into the smile he offered Chloe.

Lucie exhaled and sank back into her chair.

Why did the strong men she'd come across feel they knew better than everyone else? Lucie was tired of dealing with that attitude. Was it a man thing? Or was it just a powerful-personality thing? Her father, brothers Sam and Max, as well as Ryder, shared a number of character traits. Most of those qualities were great—the four of them were decent, hardworking and honest. But their overbearing certainty that they knew better than others wasn't among those choice traits.

Lucie didn't understand their reasoning, but she did know that approach had wreaked havoc in her life and, quite possibly, in Deanna Lyndon's life, too. It was still wreaking havoc in Lucie's life—it was blocking progress toward her future.

It also went without saying that a reunion of the siblings would likely go a long way toward helping Ryder heal. It was, after all, that broken relationship that lay at the root of his emotional scars.

Ryder's refusal to meet her gaze during the rest of their lunch emphasized what he'd already said. She didn't think she'd made him think beyond his closed attitude. But she wasn't ready to leave things as they stood. Her frustration had reached astronomical heights.

She gave it one more try, from a different angle this time. "Think about it this way. You're keeping alive a dream Dee may have put to rest years ago. If someone tried to force me into a mold I created for myself as a child, they'd be trying to turn me into a circus clown with orange fuzz hair, a rubber nose and enormous, floppy shoes."

The corner of his mouth twitched.

Good! At least a fragment of a sense of humor remained. She plowed ahead. "Trust me. Even though that's what I wanted to do with my life until about the time I turned twelve, it's the last thing I want to do these days. I think you may need to let the past stay in the past."

He pushed back his chair, threw a couple of bills on the table, then kissed the top of Chloe's head. When his blue-gray gaze met Lucie's, she shivered at the chill that ran through her. "You just don't understand."

As he strode away, Lucie had the feeling he believed she never would. Heart-deep sadness filled her.

Maybe she should listen to her own advice. Maybe she should let all those warm thoughts she'd sheltered about him over the years stay in the past as well. Maybe they didn't have a future, after all.

On his way back to the office, Ryder's mind took a turn toward the past. He landed in the middle of memories of Dee and Troy studying pictures of grand old houses, as the three of them sat in the front room of his grandparents' home, where he still lived to this day. He'd only half listened to their impractical ideas.

An unruly part of his brain reminded him of the concrete and practical suggestions Lucie had made. To Aunt Myra. There was no reason to believe she'd done otherwise with Troy. It shouldn't surprise him that mother and son had decided to go along with Lucie rather than turn to Ryder, as they'd done before.

His emotions, all in an uproar since Lucie had arrived in Lyndon Point, again surged and a pang struck in the vicinity of his chest. Ryder paused as he approached Great-great-grandfather Percy's house and took a good look at the place. He'd studied it many times in his life, heard his sister praise its details, listened to her promise to bring it back to its rightful beauty someday in the future.

But now, Lucie had landed in Lyndon Point and taken over Ryder's sister's dreams. She was even pushing Ryder aside, teaching his relatives to help themselves.

Sort of.

He should be happier, elated even.

He slipped his hands in his pockets, toed a rock out of his way, then took a couple of steps down the sidewalk. He glanced back at the empty porch, and that strange sense of loneliness came over him again.

Ryder remembered Lucie laughing at something Troy had said, and his middle clenched. Even in work clothes, her hair tied up in a messy knot, and as obstinate as ever, she appealed to him as no other woman ever had. She'd slipped into his town and his family's life with an ease that stunned him.

Did she realize what she was doing? He felt pushed aside, as though she'd displaced him from his rightful place among his relatives. Her actions made him feel…useless.

Which was ridiculous, since he'd spent a great deal of time wishing his family members would learn to stand on their own, to rely less on him and more on their own abilities. Now Lucie was showing them how to do just that. He should be grateful.

Instead, he felt hurt.

When she'd told him he had a daughter, he'd thought he was adding to his already large family. Now, even though Hurricane Lucie had been in town less than a month, he had to wonder if instead of adding to his family, she'd come to cut him right out.

He didn't need that. He couldn't stand to lose any more family connections.

There was also the matter of the house, Dee's house. Lucie wanted it. So on top of the lousy way she was making him feel about his family's dynamics, she also wanted to take over Dee's dream. How could he let her do that? How could he let her eliminate all chances of Dee ever returning to her rightful place?

And then there was Lucie herself. Ryder loved her. He'd come to accept that fact. But he'd also accepted that they'd probably never agree about much of anything. Was that any way to build a future?

Was he really as stubborn as she said? She certainly was. Could love ever surmount their inherent differences?

Chapter Fifteen

"May I come in?" Lucie asked Ryder.

She'd walked into Lyndon Accounting, checked with Wendy and, when his assistant told her he wasn't with a client, she'd gone ahead and knocked. She held her breath, waiting for his response.

He didn't make her wait long. "Sure."

Lucie closed the door behind her, wondering how he would receive what she'd come to say. It had been three days since he'd found her at Great-great-grandfather Percy's house, when she'd encouraged Troy to focus his business efforts on restoring older homes. Like the Lyndon family house.

She'd let the time pass, seeing Ryder briefly the two times when he'd stopped at the B & B to pick up Chloe. She'd spent hours and hours trying to unearth information on Deanna Lyndon, but she hadn't sniffed out anything more than what she'd learned from Ryder, Edna and Myra. Now Lucie didn't know how to process what her father had told her during his early morning call. Or her own inability to come up with additional data.

"How can I help you?" Ryder asked, formal in his tone and distant in his expression.

Did he expect everyone to ask for help when they approached him because of his line of work, or had he gone into accounting because it put him in that position? Lucie doubted he'd take a question along those lines particularly well.

She took another tack. "I didn't come for help. I came because I want to help *you,* but so far I haven't had much success."

"What do you mean?"

Lucie's stomach knotted. This wasn't going to be easy, and his determined, neutral attitude didn't help. "Let's sit. I have some things to go over with you, and then we should make some decisions."

"Some things—some decisions? I don't follow, but yes, please sit."

Lucie perched on the edge of the comfortable brown-leather wingback armchair she pulled closer to his desk. Ryder, though, spoke before she'd gathered her thoughts.

"Is this about the house again?" he asked. "Because if it is, you should know your complaint has gone through the proper channels. The house, in its current condition, has been declared a public nuisance. City Council is thrilled with your donation of landscaping." He didn't look happy.

She fought the urge to smile and left that subject for a later time. "In a roundabout way, my visit is about the house, but it's also about more than our disagreement over a weed-choked yard. I think you'll agree it's more important, too."

"Please, go ahead. I'm listening."

"It's—it's about your sister."

He straightened, shoulders rigid and squared. His expression changed, went as blank as if he'd drawn a curtain between the two of them. His eyes only hinted at his feelings. She wasn't encouraged.

But she had to go on. "After we spoke at the beach, I realized we'd never come to an agreement on the house until you have a chance to talk to your sister. You told me you'd had no luck finding her, so I—I decided to take up the search myself."

Ryder's sharp intake of breath and his tightening lips spoke loud and clear. "And?"

"And I came to tell you that—well, that I called my father to ask for his help."

"Your father? You expect him to find Dee, and then buy you the house, too?"

Lucie bit back her spurt of anger. "I've been calling the shots in my life, and Chloe's, ever since you and I parted on that beach. I don't expect anything from my father."

Her firm statement seemed to catch Ryder by surprise. She hoped she'd made her point without having to discuss her relationship with her father any further.

"I asked for his help, and he agreed to give it." She explained about her father's work and investigators. "But they haven't come up with anything yet," she said in the end. "I didn't pick up her trail, either. If we only had the boyfriend's last name—"

"He insisted he only needed one name." Ryder's voice dripped scorn. "Like Michelangelo, Leonardo, Raphael. Arrogant idiot, comparing himself to real artistic geniuses."

Or revealing himself a fan of teenaged mutant amphibian cartoon characters from the eighties.

Lucie stifled a nervous giggle. Anxiety often triggered random thoughts, but she knew Ryder well enough to tamp down the ridiculous image. Although, from what she could tell, the nutty idea did seem to fit the picture Ryder, Myra and Edna had painted of Dee's offbeat nomadic boy-friend.

She laced her hands on her lap, crossed her ankles and gave Ryder a prim smile. "The artist community hasn't heard of a budding master by the name of Maurice."

Ryder snorted. "They won't."

"That's not the point. What's important is that up to now, no one's found your sister."

He leaned forward, hands clenched, anger across his features. "Did anyone put you in charge of finding Deanna? I don't remember asking you."

"No one asked me, but you need to find her." Here came the hardest part. "A part of you seems stuck in the hurt she left behind when she took off. You need to let it go, Ryder. You need to heal."

He scoffed. "I'm not stuck. I've moved on, focused on my career and even run a successful political campaign. Now I've set goals for my tenure as mayor. That doesn't sound like a man who's stuck, does it? And I don't need you to find Dee. I've tried, and failed. What made you think you'd succeed? Besides, it's not your place to try and find her. That's for me to do. I'm her brother. I'm the one who knows her best."

"You may have known her very well once upon a time," Lucie said with a gentle smile, "but I'm speaking from personal experience. What you said right now sounded like something my dad would say. That controlling attitude pushed me away from my family, and it may be what's keeping Dee away."

At his shuttered expression, Lucie fought for and found the composure and compassion she needed to go on. "You need to face your sister, Ryder. I have a stake in finding her, too. I don't really need your permission for anything, but I'd like us to pool our efforts."

He scoffed. "I can't believe you thought you'd find her when I've failed. I spent years looking for her. What did you think you'd accomplish in a couple of days?"

She shrugged. "I'm not ready to give up yet."

"I already told you. I think Dee is scared to come back. I'm sure she'll return when she's ready to overcome her fear."

"Why would she be scared? What does she have to fear?"

"I think she's scared of our family's anger. Our relatives and I came down hard on her about her relationship with Maurice."

"So where does the house stand?"

He ran a hand through his hair, rumpling its smooth, well-groomed appearance. "The house has to be waiting for her. I have to keep alive the hope that she can still make her dream come true. Sooner or later, that dream will lure her home again."

Lucie's patience began to thin. "Sooner or later? I don't have that kind of time or endless funds. I need to move forward—just as you do. Just as Dee may have done three years ago."

Ryder let out a gust of breath. "What if you're wrong? Just consider that for a moment. What if Dee overcomes her fear of the family's anger and comes home, only to find I've turned over the house she'd always loved to the woman I—to the mother of my child? Don't you see how she'd see it as another betrayal on my part?"

She drew a deep breath. "You're right. I hadn't thought of that. All the more reason for us to find her. The sooner we do find her, the sooner you'll find peace. And we can deal with the what ifs then."

"We?"

"We both need her here." This was hard, harder even

than she'd expected, and there was still more to say. Lucie tightened her fingers to keep them from shaking. "Even Chloe needs Dee to return. Instead of arguing all the time, you and I would be best served if we joined forces to find your sister. Please, Ryder. Humor me. Let's look at this as a puzzle with missing pieces. Each missing piece is the answer to a question."

When he didn't answer, Lucie counted off fingers on her right hand. "Where is she? How is she supporting herself? Has she assumed a new identity? Did she marry Maurice? Or someone else? Is she still painting or has she gone into—oh, I don't know. Nursing, maybe."

Ryder shrugged.

"Can't you see? You don't have the answers—no more than I do. Let me help you—let's work together. In fact, while I was talking with Troy the other day, something came up that might get us somewhere."

He narrowed his eyes. "Something came up?"

Lucie ignored his skepticism. "Don't you think Dee might have found her way to an area with beautiful old homes?"

"Every town has an old home or two. That won't find her."

"Hear me out." She leaned forward, her enthusiasm taking over. "There are parts of the country that pride themselves on their historic districts. There's San Francisco, of course, but there's also Cape May in New Jersey and Charleston in South Carolina. Think of Savannah, Georgia, Galveston, Texas and a bunch of others. Have you considered that angle?"

"Old houses aren't my thing, but I've a feeling that if you check out the National Register of Historic Districts, you'll find hundreds of those areas. How's that going to find my sister?"

"Since she likes them so much, maybe she's bought a historic home and restored it. Ever think of using the register to try and find her?"

Ryder didn't answer right away.

Lucie took hope. At least he hadn't objected outright.

"There must be hundreds—no, thousands—of these homes, with thousands of owners. How am I going to sift through all that info?"

A step in the right direction. "That's where my father's investigators come in. They can check property records in a flash. Deeds are filed in courts all over the country. It's public information. You know that. You're an accountant."

Ryder leaned back into his high-back leather desk chair. He laced his hands and brought his steepled index fingers to his lips. Lucie glanced around the attractive office, unwilling to reveal how much she wanted him to agree to work with her. That would give her hope for the future. Not just for Chloe's, but Lucie and Ryder's, as well.

"I have to admit," he said, "you might have a decent idea."

Her relief exploded in a burst of sarcasm. "Oh, thanks. Such enthusiasm."

"But you have to admit, it won't be easy."

She grew serious again. "Nothing's ever been easy for me, so I don't bother to look for the easiest way. I just look for the most promising options."

He seemed to waver, and Lucie wondered if he feared finding his sister as much as he wanted to do so. Maybe in the deepest corners of his mind, he worried learning Dee had moved past her childhood dreams and left him behind. He might not be ready to accept his sister as an adult.

Lucie didn't think it would help to push him too hard. She realized that for Ryder to heal he had to be ready to set aside the past. Only then could he face the present. Only then would he step into the future.

She bit her tongue and prayed. When the silence dragged on, that bold part of her reared up its head again. "Not only do you need to find your sister," she said, her voice gentle, "but you may also need to sell that house for your own sake. It may be the anchor around your neck that's actually holding you captive to the past."

If she'd prodded him with a sharp needle, he wouldn't have bolted upright with any more oomph.

"An anchor? A captive?" He shook his head. "This isn't a pirate movie, Lucie. I don't have to sell that house at all. Besides, it belongs to Lyndon Point."

"The technicality of ownership strikes me as your preferred smokescreen. You only hold fifty percent of the deciding power, but you're withholding your vote for personal purposes. Let go of the past. Let go of the mistake you made and forgive yourself. You can't freeze that house in time, hoping your sister will come back, hoping you can set her up within its four walls and by doing that—oh, I don't know—somehow be retroactively absolved of wrongdoing."

"You don't know what you're talking about."

"Maybe I don't. But there's a chance I might. There's also the chance I may have done what you've most feared. Tell me, Ryder, did I just voice your feelings out loud?"

Before he could answer, the office door flew open and the doorknob banged into the wall.

Lucie winced.

Two teenaged girls dressed in colorful layered T-shirts and stylishly tight jeans ran in, while Wendy yelled as she bounded from behind her desk. "Hey! I told you he's busy."

"Uncle Ryder!" one of them said. "You have to help us."

Lucie didn't know whether to scream or cry. She suspected she'd only had that one chance to change Ryder's mind, and with the girls' arrival, the chance was now lost.

She stood. "I—I've taken enough of your time." She almost ran out of Ryder's office, the lump in her throat so hard and painful she struggled to breathe. "Just think about what I said."

Three hours later, Ryder left the office and headed to the Quigleys' B & B. He did so reluctantly, not quite ready to concede at least another point to Lucie. Not that they were engaged in some kind of chess game.

After she'd left, he'd had to deal with his two second cousins. Daisy and Lily had their hearts set on a cultural trip to Paris, one his cousin Bryan and his wife considered unsuitable for young teen girls. No matter how the twins had painted the excursion, Ryder had agreed with their parents. Supervision was to be minor, and the overall value of the expensive project questionable. He'd called Bryan while the girls waited, but in the end, he'd come down on the side of logic.

Who knew what might happen to teen tourists?

He knew the pain of loss, and couldn't see his cousin risking the same.

The girls hadn't been happy. They'd stomped out of the office, their disappointment morphing into anger toward him.

Then he'd tried to work. And failed. Lucie's words had buzzed in his head each time he'd opened a client file. When he hadn't been able to take it anymore, he'd gone to the waiting room and told Wendy he was done for the day.

"Look what's coming back," Wendy had answered, indicating the large front window.

The door had banged open as Daisy and Lily had burst in again to sing Lucie's problem-solving praises. It seemed, when the girls had left, Lucie had been sitting on a bench outside. Somehow the three females had begun to talk, and Lucie had yet again come up with a solution to his family's dilemma.

This time her solution had taken the form of a well-chaperoned mission trip to exotic Morocco, a trip sponsored by the church the Adams ladies had been attending with the Quigleys. Bryan and Mary were consulted, and the deal was struck.

He had to admit it was the perfect compromise.

And his relatives hadn't needed him to broker it. All Lucie had done was offer an idea. Bryan, Mary and the twins had done the rest.

Now, as he stood before the beautiful blue beach cottage the Quigleys tended with much love and care, he had to admit Lucie might be right about a few other things. He had to face her, thank her, give credit where credit was due.

But it wouldn't be easy. Not for him.

He walked up to the house and clang the shiny brass ship's bell that did the work of a doorbell. Lucie answered, to his surprise.

"I saw you out my window," she said. "I—I hope I didn't offend you earlier today."

"No offense taken, Lucie. May I come in?"

She gave a nervous little laugh and gestured toward the room at her left. "Of course. The parlor's lovely. Make yourself comfortable."

Ryder didn't know if comfortable was possible at the moment, but he did head for the generous, well-upholstered armchair. She went for the wooden rocker right to the side. Before either one of them could sit, he spoke.

"I came to thank you for what you did today. The girls are thrilled and can't stop talking about the Moroccan trip. My cousin and his wife are grateful, too, and they'll be calling you soon."

Lucie gave a tight smile. "I'm glad it worked out."

"I—um—you might be right about something else. I might be trying too hard to fix things and to keep them as they've been in my memories of better times because it's easier that way. It doesn't hurt as much."

"Oh, Ryder."

"I have a lot to think about. And pray about." He crossed to her side. "I want you to know I haven't ignored a word you've said."

She swallowed hard and Ryder saw the hint of tears in her eyes. "Thank You, Father."

"Amen," Ryder said. "And thank you, too. Seriously. For making me think, and for everything you've done for my family."

She offered him a crooked grin. "I was just in the clichéd right place at the right time."

So that was how she was going to play it. Fine. He'd go along with her. It was easier until he'd done the soul-searching he knew he had to do. The personal examination he'd already begun. "You came up with a great compromise."

"Let's see how it goes. I tried to see it from the parents' point of view." She turned and grabbed her purse from the corner of the couch. "I'm a parent, too, you know. And I'd better grab Chloe and head on out before she chatters Mrs. Quigley right out of her mind."

Ryder approached. "Please, wait a minute."

She paused.

He took her arm and drew her close. He didn't have all

the answers, but this he knew through and through. She was an amazing woman, and he wanted her near.

Near? Hah!

In his arms. For a long, long time.

This was just a start.

He hoped.

Before Lucie realized what he was about to do, Ryder wrapped his arms around her and tucked her head under his chin. His warmth welcomed her, and while she fought it, stood stiff at first, after a few minutes of closeness and the recognition of her longing for his touch, she stopped her resistance. She melted into him, wrapped her arms around him as well.

They stood like that for a long, peace-filled time, and Lucie savored Ryder's nearness. She'd longed for this. Now that she had it again, she didn't know how she would do without it. She offered up a silent prayer for God's will to be done between them, not just for Chloe's sake, but for hers and Ryder's as well.

Thoughts of Chloe yanked her back out of Ryder's spell. "I really do have to go," she said. "Chloe…"

He nodded. "Ah—could I join you?"

His question surprised her. "Sure. But we weren't doing anything special. Just walking to Tea & Sympathy. Do you like tea?"

"Even if I didn't, I'm smart enough to say I do."

Lucie chuckled. "That's one wise response."

He smiled back and followed her to the kitchen.

Since he was so positively inclined toward her at the moment, she took another bold step. "Ryder? What about what I said earlier? Are you going to block my efforts to find your sister? Will you let me try? Can we work together?"

When he didn't hurry to respond, she went on. "Please do it for Dee's sake as well as yours. For your family's sake, and even the town's. While we're at it, we do need to settle this house thing for Chloe's sake."

She held her breath, felt his warmth just a whisper away from her back.

"I…" He paused, started again. "You might be right about this, too."

She let out the breath and sagged. His broad chest supported her, and his arms held her close. "Thanks," she whispered, a tremor of emotion in her voice.

"I'm ready to move forward and see where this all leads."

Happy tears stung her lids. She slipped out of his embrace, but let him hold her close by the hand. He squeezed it gently, before he finally released her.

She reached a hand to his face, cupped his jaw, felt the sandpaper texture of his skin. It was all so familiar. He still had the power to move her. And yet, they were different people these days. "Me, too, Ryder. Me, too."

Chapter Sixteen

One morning two weeks after Lucie and Ryder reached their truce, her frustration at the lack of progress in finding Dee reached new heights. The issue threatened to consume her, even while she tried to work on the Victorian's gardens or when she helped Troy develop a new marketing plan for his architectural restoration business.

The day before, however, Troy had given her something to think about. Could Dee have sought employment in a company similar to his newly redirected enterprise? Would it be possible to track her down through a potential employer?

After all, as Troy had said, he and Dee had often talked of going into business together, she as the project designer, he as the general contractor on the job.

It was days since she'd last talked to her father, and she couldn't stand the silence on his end any longer, not now that she had a potential lead. She called.

But her dad was with a client right then. As she waited for his return call, she looked over the list of restoration specialists west of the Rockies she'd come up with after she and Troy had gone their separate ways.

Once Carter was on the line, she shared the possibility,

one which he agreed made sense. They decided that Lucie should continue her Western search, while her father's associates should look to the east.

After quick farewells, Lucie settled down to work while Chloe spent the morning with the Quigley grandchildren. Notebook by her laptop, she broke down her search first by state, then major city, followed by historical district.

Roger, Carter's P.I., called her back a short while into her investigation and explained how many who disappear tend to retain a portion of their real names when developing a new identity. In Dee's case, Roger felt she might have kept her first name, since Lyndon was distinctive and could be easily traced.

After the informative call, Lucie resumed her search and had soon come up with a list of large, medium and small firms that specialized in restoring vintage homes in her designated part of the country. She then called company after company, asking for Deanna. As she ticked off names on the list, she couldn't help but wonder if this wouldn't culminate in another dead end. Every hour, she touched base with Roger and learned that he, too, was coming up empty-handed.

That is, until she called Thornton Restoration Partners, just outside of Denver. When she asked for Deanna, instead of the usual "We have no one here by that name," she was asked to hold while she was transferred. While Lucie liked Vivaldi's "Spring" as much as the next woman, its familiar notes got on her nerves while she waited.

After precisely two minutes and forty-seven seconds, which she watched tick down on the old-fashioned, round alarm clock on the vintage dresser in her room, a feminine voice answered.

"This is Deanna Carlini. How may I help you?"

She'd found her. There couldn't be another woman

with that name, one cobbled from Dee's background. For a moment, Lucie's excitement rendered her speechless.

"Dee?" she said tentatively. "I'm helping a friend who's been looking for a woman named Deanna, a woman with a zeal for older homes and restoration. Are you…Deanna Lyndon?"

The sharp gasp spoke louder than any other response could have.

"Please," Lucie urged. "Don't hang up on me. Your family has been looking for you for a long time. They're anxious to speak to you. They don't even know you're still alive."

In a tired voice, Dee said, "Please tell them I'm fine. But I have no intention of going back to Washington State. I don't even want to talk to them, to give them another chance to pick another fight, so please forget you've spoken with me. I'll—I'll pull up and move if they try to chase me down again."

"Wait! Please don't hang up. Give me a chance to explain why I called."

Deanna didn't answer right away, and Lucie wondered if Ryder's sister was about to cut the connection and vanish. But pushing wouldn't help. She prayed, asked the Lord to soften Dee's heart.

"I'll listen," Dee finally said, "but don't think I'm going to skip home because that control-freak brother of mine wants me to."

Lucie burst into a nervous laugh. "He does have a tiny problem with control, but I never thought you'd be the kind to follow a Pied Piper big brother, either. The woman your family has described is more loyal to her goals than that."

Her words must have impressed. Dee murmured, "Hmm…"

If Lucie was ever going to get anywhere, she knew she had to step out of her comfort zone. She wasn't about to have a better chance. Soon Dee would reinforce her defenses. Lucie hoped her openness spoke to Ryder's long-lost sister.

"I'd like to tell you about myself," she said. "Maybe if you know where I'm coming from, you'll see things a little differently."

When Deanna didn't answer, Lucie went ahead. She told the story of the spring-break romance, surprising Ryder's sister when she told Dee she had a niece, and wound down with details of the move west.

"You really gave up your career to make sure Ryder had a chance to be a daddy?" Surprise and something else, admiration maybe, rang in Dee's voice.

"I'm a Christian," Lucie said. "I don't think I could have faced my Lord if I'd kept Chloe away from Ryder. I had to do what I knew was right in my Heavenly Father's sight. But trust me, it was one of the hardest things I've ever done."

"I'll say. You left everything you'd worked for behind."

"That wasn't as hard as stepping out in faith and offering to share my child with a man I didn't know—memories of a college guy on the beach don't count."

When Dee fell silent, evidently weighing what she'd heard, Lucie added, "The man I found in Lyndon Point is a mix of the college jock I met six years ago and a man devoted to his family and his town. He's also a man who needs to face the sister who ran away in anger—"

"Oh, no. No way. I told you I wasn't going to go home like a good little girl. I heard you out, now I need to get back to work."

"Please don't hang up. Let me tell you where things stand before you make up your mind."

Even though Deanna reluctantly agreed to listen, Lucie knew her time had almost run out. "Your brother blames himself for pushing you away. I don't think he'll ever heal from the guilt and pain he still feels. On the other hand, you sound as though you've been able to move on."

"Of course I have."

"Please consider meeting with him. Help him understand who you are today."

"Why are you so intent on this? Aside from the fact that Ryder is your daughter's father."

"I moved, remember? I still hope to open up my store here in town. Your aunt Edna has been looking for an affordable place that would work for my store," she said, "and we have widened our search miles out from Lyndon Point, but so far we haven't found a thing." She paused, breathed a silent prayer. "I want Chloe to grow up close to her father, but I also need to support myself. Your family home is the best chance I have. Nothing is as perfect as that beautiful old Victorian."

Dee exploded. "I can't believe that pigheaded nut is holding on to that house! Sure, I always loved it. I still think it's great. But I've built a life for myself here in Denver. I'm not going back to Lyndon Point, regardless of what Ryder wants. An old house isn't going to make me change my mind."

"Any chance you'd be willing to come out here and tell Ryder yourself? I know that's asking a lot, but there's a lot at stake. Not just for me and Chloe, but for your brother, too. He needs to see you, to hear you tell him what you just said."

"I'm not crazy about that idea. Why would he need to hear it from me? Can't he figure out that I don't want him to badger me about coming back to do whatever he wants me to do? How much louder can I speak than by staying away from the house?"

"Hearing it face-to-face might be the only way he'll let the past go."

"Oh, yes, Lucie. You are asking a lot of me." Deanna's resolute voice bore an echo of Ryder's no-nonsense strength in its feminine pitch. "I can't make that kind of commitment to you like this, so suddenly, over the phone. But I can agree to think about everything you've said. I'll call you as soon as I make up my mind."

Seconds later, the women hung up. As unsatisfactory as the outcome was, Lucie knew she had to put the future in her Heavenly Father's hands. She hoped Dee wouldn't take long to let her know.

She hoped Deanna Lyndon was ready to face her past, too.

A week later, on an otherwise normal gray and rainy Pacific Northwest day, Lucie hurried down Main Street to Lyndon Accounting. Ryder's assistant, Wendy, held the door open as Lucie closed her cheery lime-green umbrella.

"All set?" she asked Wendy.

"Oh, yeah. I can't wait for the fireworks!"

Lucie had nothing against fireworks, but she hoped things went off much better than with a crash. With a wink for Wendy, she said, "Let's do it."

Wendy stepped up to the door to Ryder's office, knocked and asked if she could come in.

"Go ahead. I'm not leaving for another twenty minutes."

If Lucie had anything to do with it, he wouldn't be leaving for a whole lot longer than that. Standing tall and with her head held high, she stepped into his office and paused next to the door.

Deanna followed. "Hi, Ryder."

He froze. Stared at his sister.

"Dee?" he asked, wonder in his voice. "You're finally home!"

Lucie slipped out of Ryder's office, leaving the siblings to share their emotional reunion in peace and privacy.

A short while later, when she heard raised voices behind the door, she glanced at Wendy, who shrugged and whispered, "Let them hash it out. It's up to them to figure out how they'll treat each other in the future."

Lucie prayed silently for the Lord's blessing on the meeting, for His healing touch, for His help in bridging the rift between Ryder and Dee. But before she'd even reached her amen, the door burst open.

Dee stormed out. "I can't believe what a stubborn block of rock you are, Ryder!" She paused in front of Wendy's desk. "He's all yours. Better you than me."

Dismay struck Lucie as Dee rushed out. What now? She'd held such high hopes for the reunion, but by no stretch of the imagination had it gone even remotely well.

She stood to follow. "I'm sorry, Wendy. I didn't think it would go that bad. Now you're stuck dealing with his bad mood."

Ryder's assistant shrugged. "They're a lot alike, you know."

"Maybe—"

"Please come into my office, Lucie," Ryder said from the doorway.

Feeling like she'd been transported back to junior high and into the principal's office, she did as Ryder asked.

He closed the door. "I want you to know I don't blame you for the way things turned out."

She squashed a snippy retort. "I did what you probably should have done years ago. I accepted your sister for who she's become. That's how I found her, you know. By tracking down her interests. Then she took the first step and came to see you, but it seems you're still stuck on your stale ideas."

He gave a dismissive wave and walked to his desk chair. "Dee's still the same flighty girl she was when she left. She threatened to leave Denver for who-knows-where if I try to talk sense to her again. She hasn't come up with an ounce of levelheaded practicality in the last three years." He shrugged. "I'm sure she'll crash and burn sooner or later, and when she does, she'll come back home where she belongs."

Lucie tamped down her disappointment. "She's not a girl anymore, but I realize it might be easier for you to see her as she once was. Change takes effort, and I'm afraid you're not ready—or is it willing?—to even try." She sighed. "Does this also mean you're going to keep that house in the disastrous condition it's in?"

Ryder walked to the window. Hands in his pockets, he stared out into the gray gloom. He didn't say a word.

Lucie struggled with the overwhelming sense of defeat, but she gave it one more try. For Chloe. For Dee. For Ryder, the man she loved.

"Did you even ask your sister what she's been doing in Denver? Did you try to understand who she is these days?"

"She does something or other at a company that restores money-pit homes."

"Ryder! Dee put herself through school. She earned a drafting certificate and then landed her job. She prepares the drawings builders use to remodel and, more importantly, restore homes. She's an accomplished woman, and supports herself quite well. That doesn't sound flighty to me."

He gave her another dose of silence.

But Lucie had reached the end of her patience. And her hope for the two of them. The ache of heartbreak hit hard. "I guess this means you're not ready to move on."

"I have a lot of work to do."

Fighting tears, she reached for the doorknob. "That's about as clear as it gets. Which leaves me in a rotten position. I have nowhere to open my store around Lyndon Point. My only alternative is to pack up Chloe's and my things and find somewhere else to go. I'll let you know when I decide—maybe I'll head to Denver. At least Chloe will have her aunt nearby. I'm sure you and I can work out an arrangement for you to spend time with her."

He spun and pinned her with his steely stare. "If you're going to wander around the country, unable to support our daughter adequately, then the responsible thing is to leave her with me. I can give her a stable life while you're out there doing your cloth design thing—"

"Is that what all this has been about? To take Chloe away from me?" Lucie's breath came out in harsh gusts, and fear turned her fisted hands into lumps of ice. "Forget it, Ryder. It's not going to happen. You're not going to put her in a cage so you can control her every move. I worked too hard to get away from that back in Connecticut. I won't let you do to our daughter what my family did to me."

"It's not my plan or intention to 'take' Chloe away from you," he said in a tired voice. "Nor do I want to put her in a cage of any kind. What I want to do is teach her a levelheaded approach to life. I can't let you drag her around with you while you go from town to town, looking for a place to set up shop."

Fear made Lucie's heart pound, made her hands turn to icy lumps. "I wouldn't have to do that if you'd change your mind. You chased your sister out of your life once, and from what I can see, you're about to do it again. Now you're pushing me to earn a living somewhere else." Fighting panic, she kept her voice level but firm. "Our daughter comes with me, Ryder. It's what's best for her, and you know it."

"An erratic, wandering lifestyle is not the best for Chloe."

"Then agree with City Council and sell me the house."

"I can't choose between my sister and my child."

"This is just too sad. You can't—or maybe won't—see the truth. You don't have to choose between them. The choice is between your misguided need to atone for a past mistake and restoring your relationship with Dee, then stepping up to be a real father to Chloe."

"That's insane, Lucie. I'm not doing any kind of atonement. Of course I want a relationship with both Chloe and Dee."

"It looks like unnecessary guilt to me. But the truth, Ryder, is that you don't have to do any atoning on your own. God's already provided for that with His Son's sacrifice on the cross. Don't make that irrelevant for you. Ask Dee to forgive you for your stubborn big-brother tendencies. Forgive yourself for pushing her away. Let the past go. Take a step into the future. Step out in faith. God's ready for you. So are Chloe and Dee."

Lucie stepped toward him, fully vulnerable, but unable to do otherwise. She held out a hand, which he let hang between them. For a moment, he looked at her fingers, at her face, that longing she'd noticed before in the depths of his eyes.

Her heart picked up its beat.

He turned away.

Hope crushed, she went ahead and said what she had to say. "I'm waiting for you, too."

"Work, Lucie. I have clients who count on me. I have to do what they've hired me to do."

The pain in her chest grew more acute. She'd thought her heart had broken six years before. Now, with a daughter between them, and that daughter's future in the balance, she knew a more exquisite quality of pain.

"I got it," she said. "Don't bother saying it again."

She stumbled out, blinded by scalding tears. In the waiting room, she grabbed her bright lime-green umbrella and, without a word to Wendy, yanked open the door. She ran into the light rain. The cold drops stung her heated skin.

She'd been a fool to think she and Ryder could build on the moments of closeness they'd recently shared. A leftover attraction and shared parenthood were not the stuff on which futures were built. It was time to move on.

Where to? Lucie didn't know. She hoped God would show her before she stuck around long enough to let Ryder break her heart a third time.

Chapter Seventeen

Three hours later, Ryder flung his pen down on the desk and rubbed his face with his hands. Lucie was right about one thing. He couldn't see a way for them to agree on anything. It wouldn't be fair to foist that on Chloe.

What was he supposed to do? Let the two of them leave Lyndon Point? Never see his daughter again?

A pang struck his heart. He'd come to love Chloe in the brief time they'd spent together. It warmed his heart every time she said she loved him or called him Mr. Daddy.

And that made it tougher to find any measure of peace. He didn't have an answer to the million questions in his head. What was best for a child who hadn't known her father until just a few weeks before? A child who'd always depended on her mother? How could they explain a mother and father who'd never spent more than a handful of days together? Parents who argued regularly in each other's company?

That couldn't be the best environment for raising a child.

If Lucie and Chloe left, Chloe would find a new candidate for daddy in no time.

The thought hurt. How would he feel months, maybe

years from now, when he learned that Lucie had married, had given Chloe that daddy she wanted so much, and it wasn't him?

How would he feel when he learned Lucie loved another man?

And yet, if he let Lucie buy the house he'd have to give up hope of helping Dee when she came back home.

Sure. Dee said she was happy drawing pictures of patched-up houses that probably needed to be razed. But that was only a fad. The "historic homes" frenzy would soon die down, and everyone would come to their senses. Houses reached the end of their useful lives at some point. When they did, the best thing to do was to tear them down, and rebuild for the future.

When that truth affected Dee's chances of employment, he would have a property ready for her. He knew his sister would be too stubborn to accept the end of beat-up old wrecks' popularity. In Great-great-grandfather Percy's home, Dee would find the place to settle down, regroup, restore at will and eventually find a rational path forward.

Ryder wasn't ready to give up that dream. Even if Dee had insisted she wanted nothing to do with Lyndon Point or the Victorian on Main and Sea Breeze Way.

He knew his sister better than she knew herself.

Didn't he?

As Lucie's words returned to haunt him, a twinge of discomfort twisted his guts, but he stood, turned the lights off and closed the door in his wake. He nodded to Wendy but didn't say a word. She'd taken part in Lucie's plot by letting Dee stay at her place. She should have known better than to help ambush him.

He knew what was right. He knew what his sister needed. And he'd come to a decision about Chloe's needs. He was the one with the levelheaded approach to life. He could see the practical side of the situation and could best choose what should happen next.

At the corner of Main and Sea Breeze Way, on the outside of the rusty iron fence, Ryder came to a halt and stared at the house. Could he really do that? Could he really give up his child? Could he give up all hope of a future with the only woman he had ever loved?

He put foot before foot, over and over again, his decision final. He knew what was best.

Even if saying goodbye to Chloe would be heartrending.

Even if watching Lucie walk away again would tear apart the last intact pieces of his heart.

The next afternoon, Chloe ran back to where Ryder sat on a piece of driftwood. "Here's 'nother good one," she said, holding up a fist-sized gray rock. "I like it."

"You have a good eye." Ryder held out the plastic bucket he'd bought for their walks on the beach. "It is a nice one. Pile it in."

"You're a great rock-hounder, Daddy. I like rock-hounding with you."

At the sound of that precious word, minus the *mister* that had up until then accompanied it, Ryder's heart swelled before he forced the emotion into the corner where he'd already stuffed his feelings for Dee. He couldn't afford to let his love for his little girl deepen any more. He was going to say goodbye in the near future, and he didn't know how he'd survive when she left.

But it would be best for her to go with Lucie.

He gave her a bland response. "I like rock-hounding with you, too."

Fifteen minutes later, he'd warned Chloe against getting her sandaled feet wet, kept her from running on the rocky beach and hauled around her bucket of rocks as she weighed the merits of every common pebble that caught her eye.

As mundane as the outing was, Ryder treasured every minute, knowing they'd become gems of joy in the future. Their value would increase with distance between them.

Although the pain was almost more than he could bear, he'd come to accept that Lucie was right. He couldn't wrest Chloe from her. Even though in some ways he could offer Chloe something better than another wrenching move, mother and daughter had a bond he couldn't replace.

His child barely knew him. To his bitter regret.

When he could no longer stand the circular thoughts another minute, he stood. "I'm hungry. Let's go to the Nest. I hear their chicken nuggets are especially good today."

Chloe skipped back to his side and took his bucket-less hand. "They have good barber cube sauce, too."

On their way to the diner, Chloe kept up a steady stream of chatter. She discussed flowers, her pink sandals, *Phineas and Ferb*'s latest escapade and Lucie's attempts to bake Mrs. Quigley's mouthwatering recipe for lemon poppy-seed muffins.

"They were liddle-liddle and tasted funny," Chloe said. "Mama didn't do it right. Mrs. Wiggly's muffins are enormous! And they're yummy, too."

"I love Mrs. Quigley's baked goods. She's a good one to learn from. I'm sure your mama will get it right soon."

"I hope so, 'cuz Mama says we're moving." She turned worried blue-gray eyes up to his face. "But I don't wanna go, Daddy. Not unless you come with us. Will you? Will you come with Mama and me?"

If he'd considered the pain before intolerable, he didn't know how to describe this new level of hurt. "It's not that easy, Chloe. This is where I live."

"But I love you, Daddy." Tears welled in her eyes. "I like Mrs. Wiggly, too. And I like when she takes me to play with her Haley and Isaac and Willy. If you can't come, then I want to stay here. Can you help me? Ask Mama to stay—pleeeese?"

Chloe's innocent words twisted the pain he carried in his chest. He sucked in a sharp breath, but the air seemed to stick in a knot at his throat.

It really was up to Ryder whether Lucie and Chloe left. The house…

But he couldn't ask Lucie to stay. For her to stay, he'd have to give up his hope of restoring his family.

"I can't tell your mama what to do," he finally told Chloe. "She's the one who has to decide what's…" He swallowed hard. "What's best for her. And you."

His words sounded hollow, but he hoped they'd satisfy Chloe.

As he suspected, they didn't. "Mama told Ms. Dee it's all 'cuz of a mule. D'you know where the mule is? I want to see a mule. Mama says it won't move, so she can't buy the pretty big house. Can you help me move the mule, Daddy? You're awfully big."

How could he tell his daughter she was holding hands with the mule? That he was the mule standing in her mother's way?

Fortunately for him, they'd reached the diner. "We'll see about the mule some other time. Now it's time for chicken nuggets."

But in spite of the appeal of her favorite food, Chloe kept up the chatter about the mule as she munched on the nuggets and spooned up the applesauce on the side. When done, she turned a hope-filled smile on him.

"Dessert?" she said. "I ate every bite."

"What would you like?"

"Raz scary pie!"

After spending a number of afternoons with Chloe, Ryder had become an expert at deciphering her mispronunciations. "Raspberry pie it is. Want some vanilla ice cream with it?"

"Yummy!"

Chloe finished about a third of the raz scary pie. Ryder cleaned her mouth, paid the bill, picked up the rock bucket and helped the little girl out the door.

"Good lunch?" he asked.

"The best! Can we have lunch at the Nest every day?"

Another sting. "That's up to your mama."

"I'm gonna ask her when we get to Mrs. Wiggly's house."

Her request made him wonder how much time he had left to spend with Chloe before Lucie picked up and left. And Lucie...

He'd avoided her every time he'd picked up Chloe. He didn't want to spend more time with her, not when there was no future for them. He couldn't afford more pain. He'd lost Lucie once, and he was about to lose her again.

Just as he was losing his sister for a second time. His dream of a restored family would go with Dee as soon as she took off again.

What was it about him and the women in his life? They all left, and his loneliness grew.

"Has your mama said when you're leaving Lyndon Point?" he asked.

"No, but I been praying 'bout it all the time. Mama says God listens, and He likes to give us the 'sires of our hearts." Chloe's sweet face took on a serious cast. "My heart 'sires to stay."

What could he say to that? But she didn't give him a

chance to speak. She kept going, her words like needles aimed straight at where they would hurt the worst.

"Daddy? Isaac and Willy and Haley have a mommy and a daddy. And they all live here. Real close to Mrs. Wiggly. Can you find a big old house? Mama needs one for her fabric and needles and *fff-fimble* store. And for us. If you find a big old house, then you and Mama and I can live together and we can be like them."

He already had a big old house.

Ryder's conscience stung at the admission. "It's not so easy, Chloe. Marriage is a very important, serious thing. Your mama can't just stay with me because I have a big old house. There are things like getting along—and love. It's complicated."

"I love you. Don't you love me?"

"Oh, Chloe. Of course I love you. You're my little girl."

"What 'bout Mama? Don't you like her?"

He loved her. "Ah…it's…different. It's not like finding a house and putting a daddy and a mommy in the house. It's complicated."

"I love you, and I still need a daddy. I been trusting Jesus, like Mama and Mrs. Wiggly say. But I don't *want* to trust Him, not 'bout leaving. I been waiting and waiting for my daddy, and I found you. I'm tired of all that waiting. Don't want to wait anymore."

"I understand about waiting. I've been waiting for my sister to come home for a long time."

Chloe wrinkled her nose. "I thought Auntie Dee was your sister. She's eating muffins with Mama at Mrs. Wiggly's house. She says she's home. You don't have to wait anymore."

Dee was in Lyndon Point, but she wasn't home. Not while she still planned to return to Denver. "It's complicated," he said yet again. "I can't explain."

"Mrs. Wiggly says com—complications are cuz people don't think God can fix things. She says people need to let Him do His job in Heaven. It's not so hard. I want a daddy, and you're my daddy but you don't want Mama and me and a big old house. Maybe Jesus has a daddy for me where Mama wants to move."

Ryder's heart stuttered, and he found it hard to breathe.

"C'mon. I want to go see if Mama's ready to move. If I can't have you be my daddy, then I want to find that other daddy God's got for me."

This other-daddy business had to stop. Ryder couldn't stand it. He didn't want his daughter looking at every man she met, weighing his merits, wondering if he might do as a daddy.

Ryder was her daddy.

But you're also the mule in Lucie's way.

He stood still. Yes, his commitment to Dee and her dream was a driving force in his life. But...

Had letting the house become a public eyesore brought Dee home?

Lucie had brought his sister home. She'd succeeded where he'd failed.

Lucie found Dee through my sister's love of historical homes. She knew Dee better than I.

Did she? Were the two of them so alike?

No. They couldn't be. Lucie, an artistic type, had learned a thing or two about business realities. His aunt and his cousin were benefiting from her expertise.

When I last saw her on the beach in Baja I thought of her as a flighty artist. If she can change, can't Dee also change? You can't call it both ways.

"Daddy?" Chloe asked as he dropped down on one of the iron benches downtown. "Is your tummy okay?"

"My tummy's fine." But his heart wasn't. "It's a nice

day. I want to sit in the sun for a while. Here's your bucket of rocks. You can look at them while we rest."

That was dumb. What was she going to do with the rocks while they sat on a bench? She couldn't build a pyramid in the middle of the sidewalk. He wasn't even making five-year-old sense.

No wonder Chloe was giving him a questioning stare. But he had to think, and he couldn't stand another message from his mutinous conscience.

Because the messages are right. I'm wrong—been wrong all along. I have a control problem. Like Lucie says.

The mutiny continued. And it hit hard. Was he really the control freak Dee had called him? He didn't think so. He just knew how to solve problems, he was a practical man and life needed a practical approach.

Practical doesn't mean rejecting your sister's changing goals.

Was Lucie right? Had Dee matured as much as she believed?

Only one way to know.

He had to take the next step. He had to admit he'd been wrong three years ago. And again two days before. For that matter he'd been wrong to keep silent and let Lucie go six years beforehand.

He stood and held out his hand to Chloe. "It's time to head back to Mrs. Quigley's." He set up a brisk pace. "Your mama and I have to talk."

And the first thing I have to do is admit I was wrong about the house.

He didn't want to push Lucie away a second time.

At the B & B, Ryder left Chloe in the kitchen with Mrs. Quigley, then went to the sunroom, where their hostess said he'd find Lucie, where she'd been since Dee had gone back to Wendy's place. He found her sitting at a round cast-iron-and-glass table at the far end of the room, poring over a mass of papers. She didn't notice his arrival until he closed the glass French doors and approached.

Ryder cleared his throat. "I'm sorry to disturb you."

He winced. That was no way to start a conversation. He sounded like he'd been starched and pressed.

Lucie shrugged. "I'm trying to see if I can afford a Victorian cottage for sale outside Atlanta. It's bigger than the one Edna showed me, and it looks like it might work for Chloe and me."

Atlanta? Time to face his mistakes.

"Ah…Lucie? Um…that's why I'm here. I—ah—owe you…" He ran a hand across his forehead where perspiration dampened his skin. He hurried ahead. "I owe you an apology."

Her eyes opened wide. "Excuse me?"

Ryder glanced at his feet, shuffled a bit, stuck his hands in his pockets and finally looked up and out the window at the waters of the sound. "You were right. And I'm sorry."

Lucie stood and crossed her arms. "Care to elaborate on that point? What was I so right about that it brings you here like a scolded puppy?"

"Chloe told me you have a mule in your way. I took a good look at myself and everything you've accomplished since you arrived in Lyndon Point. That mule doesn't much like what he saw."

The corner of Lucie's mouth twitched. "And…?"

"And I didn't respect Dee's wishes three years ago. She was twenty years old, an adult and…" The next part was the hardest so far. "It seems she'd outgrown her dreams for Great-great-grandfather Percy's house."

"Don't you think you should tell her rather than me?"

"I'll do that, but you're looking in Atlanta for a house. And Chloe's talking about finding a new daddy. You don't have to go that far, Lucie. Neither one of you. It really does make sense for you to fulfill your dream. This mule is moving out of your way. You can restore the house, turn it into your store and move into it with Chloe as soon as you want."

She raked his face with a piercing gaze. "Am I in the twilight zone? What brought on this radical change? Is it real?"

"As real as our little girl. I can't stand the thought of losing her, Lucie." He stepped closer. "And I can't stand the thought of letting you walk away again."

"Me?"

"Yes, you. You're the only woman I've ever loved. I've never told you that, but it's the truth. In Baja, we didn't know enough to talk, to open up to each other. We were young—stupid and young. I don't want to do that again."

Her neutral expression didn't change, and fear filled Ryder's heart. He'd opened up to her, exposed his feelings, but he still didn't know how she felt. This could go downhill in a second or less.

"I'm not sure I buy this epiphany of yours. You've stuck like a glob of glue to your narrow view of life. As recently as two days ago you refused to welcome Dee when she took the first step. Now you tell me you're sorry you've fought me like a bear over the house. That you don't want me to walk away. How am I supposed to know what to believe?"

Hope flickered. "Test me. Buy the house, fix it up. Stay around and let me spend time with you and Chloe. I have a long way to go before neither you nor Deanna will call me a control freak again, but I have to start somewhere."

"A long way is right."

"You've helped me come this far." He took the last step, and when he stood inches away, he placed his hands on her shoulders, met her gaze. "Please help me go the distance. Help me along the way. Let me help you fulfill your dream."

"Maybe Chloe's the one you need. She's the one who called you a mule to your face."

He arched a brow. "She was only repeating your words. You've taught our daughter well. She trusts what you say, and you've taught her to trust in God."

"What exactly do you want from me?"

"I want the chance to see if we have a future. I want to see if we can give Chloe the family she wants. Mama, Daddy and Chloe sounds pretty good to me."

Lucie met his gaze, questions still in the hazel depths. Then she lifted her hand to touch his face. She ran a finger along the line of his jaw, rubbing against its sandpapery feel.

"I—I owe you the same kind of honesty. You're the only man I've ever loved. I'm not sure of anything right now, but I would like to give us time. And I still want to open my store in that beautiful house."

He brought his forehead to hers. "Call Aunt Edna. Have her write up a contract. Present it to City Council at the meeting next week. I'll be the first to sign the dotted line."

"And Dee?"

He stiffened. "I'll speak to Dee. I don't know how that's going to go, but I will give the two of us a chance to put our family back together again."

"Do you want to tell Chloe the mule is ready to be a dad?"

"That's *Daddy,* I'll have you know. I've been promoted

from 'mister' as of this day." He relaxed, drew Lucie closer to his heart. "I'm ready. More than ready."

She leaned back. "Then let's head to the kitchen."

"There's something else I need to do first."

"What—"

He cut off her question with his lips.

Epilogue

"Smile!"

The flash of a camera blinded Lucie momentarily. "Enough, Nettie. You need to photograph the store, not me."

"Uh-uh, Lucie," the reporter for the local paper said. "I need a picture for the social column. There's that engagement ring to report on. Give us a look."

Lucie held out her left hand. Her heart tripped an extra beat, as it had every time she'd looked at the ruby surrounded with tiny diamonds. The tangible evidence of the pledge she and Ryder had exchanged meant more to her than just gemstones and gold.

"Okay. That's legit," she said, holding out her hand. Nettie clicked away. After a dozen or so flashes, Lucie was ready to move on. "Now that you have the picture, can you focus on the store? A new business needs all the publicity it can get."

Nettie turned to snap photos of the rainbow of fabrics in floor-to-ceiling cubicle shelves, of the tables stacked high with bolts of muslin, bags of batting and assorted cutting tools. She also took shots of the seasonal display Lucie had set up, beautiful in its Christmas shades of forest green, wine red, silver and gold, and mounds of white cloth surrounding it all.

With a nod to Lucie, Nettie slipped into the former dining room, where the clicking continued. Her yarn selection would be featured in Nettie's piece as well. Lucie had to make sure to ask Nettie for copies of the pictures and permission to use them when promoting the store.

No more than ten minutes later, the middle-aged woman was back. "Okay, Lucie. I took the pictures you wanted. Now let's talk about the news you've made."

Ryder came up behind Lucie. "You do that, Nettie. I'll focus on the storekeeper." He nuzzled her neck, then kissed her temple. "I can answer the questions for you—I'll even give you the scoop on the ceremony. It'll be next July, out in the tiki hut on the Quigleys' beach. Pastor Mark from Calvary Chapel will officiate. The bride's father, an East Coast attorney, will give the bride away, and my sister has agreed to stand up for Lucie."

Nettie shoved her glasses up her nose. "Deanna's coming home?"

"She's here this week, and she'll be back for the wedding," Ryder said. "But her life is in Denver these days. She'll take a week of vacation, then get back to her career."

Nettie scribbled on her notepad. "Now that I have you here, let me ask you this. You first, Ryder. How did it feel to find out you were a daddy when your baby's already five years old? And how about you, Lucie? How did it feel to share your child after all those years? Everyone in town's curious, and I can't leave without asking you both."

"It hasn't been easy," Ryder said, "but it's wonderful, too. We made mistakes in the past, but by the grace of God, we're doing better these days."

"Hey, Lucie!" a man yelled from the stairs. "Where do you want this box labeled Homeland Alpaca Worsted?"

Chloe chattered, "Yeah, Mama, Uncle Sammy needs to know. I'm helping him, right?"

"That's right, squirt."

Lucie smiled at her oldest brother. "Sorry, Sam. Alpaca goes in the storage room on the third floor. A lot of stairs, I know."

"No kidding," Sam said. "Where's Max?"

Ryder laughed. "Lucky man, Max. He's at Tony's picking up the pizza for the open house. Mrs. Carlini's not about to let him out until she knows the tiniest details of his life."

Lucie shook her head. "That's Max for you. My brothers have spent their lives arguing over his ability to avoid the most unpleasant jobs. One of these days it'll catch up to him. But today he gets fed, and he does love pizza."

"Me, too," Chloe said. "'Specially pep 'n ronni."

Nettie laughed and slapped her notebook closed. "Congratulations on the store and the engagement. Will you be ready for the opening in an hour?"

"I'm ready, Nettie."

Lucie knew she spoke the truth. She was ready for everything God sent her way.

She thanked the Father round the clock for all He'd given her. She and Ryder were building their future, trusting God for His guidance along the way. They had Chloe, their precious gem. Her father and brothers had left the firm in the hands of capable junior partners, and taken a family vacation for the opening of Vintage Threads.

Even though differences still existed between them, for the first time Lucie felt like a part of her family, even though she now lived across the continent. Ryder and

Deanna, too, were working to mend the rift that had kept the siblings apart for so long.

Lucie had found the best of friends in Dee.

The future looked good. God's promises gave her unending hope.

"What are you thinking?" Ryder asked.

"I'm counting my blessings."

"Mine began to shower down when God led you to Lyndon Point. I love you, Lucie."

"I love you, too."

He kissed her, and a round of applause rose around them.

She leaned back to see the circle of family and friends who'd started arriving. They'd promised to help her with the grand opening of her store.

Tears filled her eyes, happy tears. She was home. In Lyndon Point she'd found the future she'd envisioned. But most important of all, in Lyndon Point she'd found Ryder and his love.

* * * * *

Dear Reader,

I'm a true believer in second chances, and I know our merciful God is the generous giver of those precious second chances. Who doesn't wish at times for a do-over button for their life?

I loved writing Ryder and Lucie's story because their mistake had the greatest of consequences: a daughter. I always try to imagine myself in my characters' situations. Like Lucie, I would have wanted to do what was best for my child. I'm the mother of four boys. My husband and I have been married for thirty-four years, and raising my boys has brought me the greatest challenges of my life.

It was during those challenging times that I had no other recourse but to trust God and His promises. At times I could see no light at the end of the tunnel. But our loving Heavenly Father carried me in His comforting arms.

My hope is that you're encouraged by this story, and I pray that you place yourself in the Father's merciful care.

I love hearing from my readers. Your words encourage me, especially when I'm at a tough spot in my current book. I answer each letter, and appreciate the consideration you show me by taking the time to write. You can always reach me at ginnyaiken@gmail.com or through Love Inspired Books.

Thank you so very much for choosing *The Daddy Surprise*.

I pray God blesses you richly.

Questions for Discussion

1. Lucie created a different persona for herself during her spring break, acting like the free spirit she longed to be. Have you ever felt the need to escape, even if for a short period of time, from the pull of your everyday responsibilities?

2. If you could pull up roots like Lucie and move somewhere else, where would you choose to go? What is the draw of that locale?

3. As parents, we always strive to do the best for our children. How far out of your comfort zone, either literally or figuratively, would you move for your child's sake?

4. While Lucie chafed under her family's protective nature, Ryder thrived and to a certain degree derived his identity from being needed by his family members. Who do you resemble more? Why?

5. Ryder clung to his vision of his sister's dream, while Lucie clung to her vision of the perfect store. Both were extremely stubborn in their stances. Are you clinging to an old dream? If so, is it because it's a reasonable goal or are you holding on because it offers the comfort of the familiar? Are you working toward the goal? If not, why not?

6. Lucie wanted to open her quilt and needle arts store in an old home because she felt the vintage surrounding would offer the best "flavor" with which to surround

her wares. Do you fall on the side of those who dream of restoring an older home or do you shudder at the thought? What kind of surroundings do you think would give you the best chance to shine? Why?

7. The Pacific Northwest is famously—some would say notoriously—unique. What makes your part of the country famous or unique?

8. When Lucie gave Ryder the photo album she'd made for him, he was moved to tears by the images of their infant daughter. That display of emotion made her realize how much she still loved him. If you'd been Lucie's friend, would you have encouraged her to go for a renewed relationship with Ryder or would you have cautioned her against being hurt again?

9. In what ways did Ryder also have to step out of his comfort zone and start all over again?

10. What kind of change would be more difficult for you? Would you prefer to move to a new region or would you prefer to rebuild your self-image?

11. To make her point to her overprotective father and brothers, Lucie cuts all communication with them when she leaves the East Coast. Would you ever see yourself in that kind of situation? Do you think it took courage to do what she did?

12. Ryder needed to face Deanna so that he could leave the past behind. Lucie knew that meeting between the siblings was necessary if she and Ryder were ever to have a future. But she also had to face her past, and

she did so by talking to her father. Have you had to deal with a difficult and painful part of your past in order to step into your future? How did it feel?

13. In the end, Lucie and Ryder both reached out to their family members and worked to repair the various broken bonds. How do you think they fared? Do you think they had a smooth road ahead?

14. Family dynamics are minefields. Are you estranged from someone in your family? What would it take for you to take the first step to restore that relationship?

15. Children often see things far more clearly than adults do. Chloe wants a daddy. Ryder is her daddy. Lucie is her mommy. They belong together. As Christians, we're supposed to approach faith with the simple trust of a child. Have you ever had a child point out the simple reality in a situation you considered complex? Were you able to trust God? How was the situation resolved?

INSPIRATIONAL

Inspirational romances to warm your heart & soul.

TITLES AVAILABLE NEXT MONTH

Available July 26, 2011

WYOMING SWEETHEARTS
The Granger Family Ranch
Jillian Hart

THE SHERIFF'S RUNAWAY BRIDE
Rocky Mountain Heirs
Arlene James

FAMILY BY DESIGN
Rosewood, Texas
Bonnie K. Winn

FIREMAN DAD
Betsy St. Amant

ONCE UPON A COWBOY
Pamela Tracy

AT HOME IN HIS HEART
Glynna Kaye

LICNM0711

REQUEST YOUR FREE BOOKS!

2 FREE INSPIRATIONAL NOVELS
PLUS 2
FREE
MYSTERY GIFTS

YES! Please send me 2 FREE Love Inspired® novels and my 2 FREE mystery gifts (gifts are worth about $10). After receiving them, if I don't wish to receive any more books, I can return the shipping statement marked "cancel." If I don't cancel, I will receive 6 brand-new novels every month and be billed just $4.49 per book in the U.S. or $4.99 per book in Canada. That's a saving of at least 22% off the cover price. It's quite a bargain! Shipping and handling is just 50¢ per book in the U.S. and 75¢ per book in Canada.* I understand that accepting the 2 free books and gifts places me under no obligation to buy anything. I can always return a shipment and cancel at any time. Even if I never buy another book, the two free books and gifts are mine to keep forever.

105/305 IDN FEGR

Name _____ (PLEASE PRINT) _____

Address _____ Apt. # _____

City _____ State/Prov. _____ Zip/Postal Code _____

Signature (if under 18, a parent or guardian must sign)

Mail to the **Reader Service:**
IN U.S.A.: P.O. Box 1867, Buffalo, NY 14240-1867
IN CANADA: P.O. Box 609, Fort Erie, Ontario L2A 5X3

Not valid for current subscribers to Love Inspired books.

**Are you a subscriber to Love Inspired books
and want to receive the larger-print edition?
Call 1-800-873-8635 or visit www.ReaderService.com.**

* Terms and prices subject to change without notice. Prices do not include applicable taxes. Sales tax applicable in N.Y. Canadian residents will be charged applicable taxes. Offer not valid in Quebec. This offer is limited to one order per household. All orders subject to credit approval. Credit or debit balances in a customer's account(s) may be offset by any other outstanding balance owed by or to the customer. Please allow 4 to 6 weeks for delivery. Offer available while quantities last.

Your Privacy—The Reader Service is committed to protecting your privacy. Our Privacy Policy is available online at www.ReaderService.com or upon request from the Reader Service.

We make a portion of our mailing list available to reputable third parties that offer products we believe may interest you. If you prefer that we not exchange your name with third parties, or if you wish to clarify or modify your communication preferences, please visit us at www.ReaderService.com/consumerschoice or write to us at Reader Service Preference Service, P.O. Box 9062, Buffalo, NY 14269. Include your complete name and address.

Love Inspired®
SUSPENSE

RIVETING INSPIRATIONAL ROMANCE

Six-year-old Alex hasn't said one word since his mother was murdered, and now the killer has targeted Alex—and his devoted uncle raising him, Dr. Dylan Seabrook. DEA agent Paige Ashworth is on the case, but Dylan's strength and fierce love for his nephew soon have Paige longing to join their family. First, though, they must catch a killer who wants little Alex to never speak again.

Agent Undercover
by LYNETTE EASON

ROSE MOUNTAIN
REFUGE

Available in August wherever books are sold.

Love Inspired

When Kylie Jones catches her fiancé kissing another girl moments before their wedding, she runs— smack into Deputy Sheriff Zach Clayton! Zach is very understanding to her distress, but he's only in town temporarily. Unless Kylie can lead the love-shy lawman to the wedding they've *both* always dreamed of…

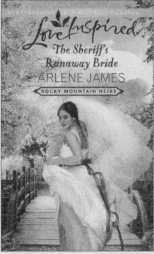

The Sheriff's Runaway Bride
by Arlene James

◄ ROCKY MOUNTAIN HEIRS ►

Available August wherever books are sold.

www.LoveInspiredBooks.com

LI87686